Walking Shadows

Walking Shadows

Modena Gelien

ACCENT BOOKS
Denver, Colorado

 MEMBER OF
EVANGELICAL CHRISTIAN
PUBLISHERS ASSOCIATION

ACCENT BOOKS
A Division of Accent-B/P Publications, Inc.
12100 W. Sixth Avenue
P.O. Box 15337
Denver, Colorado 80215

Copyright © 1978 Accent-B/P Publications, Inc.
Printed in U.S.A.

Library of Congress Catalog Card Number: 77-91491

ISBN 0-916406-90-3

To my daughter,
Shirley Cook,
author of *Diary of a Fat Housewife*,
who offered valuable
criticism in her
own sweet way.

1

Carla Preston bolted upright in bed, a scream stifled in her throat. Then, dropping back on the pillow, she pulled the covers up under her chin.

That persistent nightmare! How many times this week? And always the same—down to the minutest detail.

She propped herself up and reached for a cigarette. Seized by a coughing attack, she smashed it out. With her throat still burning, the fear of lung cancer crossed her mind—again. What a way to start a new day—nightmares and lung cancer!

Now if I were a psychoanalyst—. She mused over the details of the nightmare. Why did she always find herself alone in a strange place? Because I *am* alone, except for Penny, of course.

And that shadowy figure luring her on, but always out of reach—who could it be? The man of her dreams, no doubt. And the stairway where he disappeared before she got beyond the first step—what could that mean?

So, she wasn't a psychoanalyst. She dismissed the thought with a wave of the hand.

This is a beautiful morning, she thought. As she remembered the events of yesterday, she took another cigarette. She had done the right thing, she was sure. Putting the house and her small business up for sale had been done on impulse. But, why not? That's the way she did everything.

Carla Preston had made a decision. The life she had been living for the last five years must stop. She was fed up with everything. Excessive drinking, smoking too much. The same old crowd; shallow, brazen women; dissipated, repulsive men. If she ever hoped to regain her self-respect, she must leave this small-town atmosphere and start over. It had to be now. She couldn't start any younger.

A lump caught in her throat as her eyes swept the spacious bedroom. Yellow sunbeams filtered through white, filmy curtains, casting golden rays across the king-sized bed. Herb Preston had insisted that all the furniture in their home be solid and impressive. Everything he had said and done was solid and impressive.

Fifteen years of marriage to Herb had been a grueling display of pretended harmony—all for the sake of rapid promotions, which came at regular intervals until he reached the top.

Herb Preston's relentless climb toward success had taken its toll. His self-inflicted pressures had resulted in a coronary thrombosis, leaving Carla a widow at thirty-five.

At first she was stunned; then, with a sense of relief, she accepted the responsibilities of maintaining a home for Penny, her teenage daughter.

As if in response to her thoughts, Penny's blonde head peeked around the door.

"Happy birthday to you!" she chirped.

"Oh, no!" Carla moaned. "I knew there was a reason to stay in bed all day." She threw off the covers and slid to the edge of the bed. Penny plopped down beside her.

"Would you like your breakfast in bed?"

"Of course not. I'm not a hundred yet!"

Dragging a long box from under her bed, she lifted a new robe from reams of tissue paper. She wrapped herself in it, stepped into matching slippers, and fashion-modeled across the room.

"A little birthday present I got for myself," she smiled. "Adds a little interest to the old body, don't you think?"

"Oh, Mom, it's beautiful! Gorgeous! Dreamy!"

Before the full-length mirror in the bathroom, Carla called back to Penny, "Not bad for forty." Then she added, "Just give me a few minutes for a shower. And, while you're waiting, I like my eggs basted, bacon crisp, and coffee black."

Closing the door, she slid her hands down the satin robe. It's smooth, glossy texture high-lighted the soft curves of her body. The royal-blue color shimmered in her royal-blue eyes. It really did something for her, she mused.

Sudden tears blurred her mirrored image. What a shallow life she'd led! Seeking, always seeking something to fill her empty heart. Oh, the hopelessness of finding the right man! What a fool she was to continue the search! Resolutely she brushed the tears away. She would be happy today!

In less than five minutes she was out of the shower and into a bright paisley jumpsuit. A sheer blue scarf caught up her damp curls in a ponytail.

After applying a tint of color to lips and cheeks and a little eye shadow, she lifted herself to her full five-feet-two and smiled at her reflection.

Carla Preston, tough yet vulnerable, marched down the hall, past the long living and dining rooms and into the kitchen.

"Oh, what a beautiful morning," she sang at the top of her voice.

Penny had set the breakfast table with their best china and silver. A low vase of bachelor buttons matched the dark blue tablecloth. The tempting aroma of frying bacon and steaming coffee, along with Penny's enthusiasm, gave Carla a renewed sense of confidence and hope.

"Everything's simply lovely." She touched Penny's cheek. "You'll make someone a wonderful wife someday."

"It's funny you'd say that, Mom." Carla saw Penny's face flush. "I wanted to tell you last night, but I couldn't wait up for you." Her voice crescendoed, "Last night Ray asked me to marry him."

A dark shadow draped the room, blurring Carla's vision. Her cup began to shake. She put it down and clasped her hands in her lap.

"He wants us to be married right away. Not tomorrow or anything like that, but in a few weeks at the most," Penny continued.

How could she stop Penny's words? If she didn't answer, just ignored it, maybe everything would be as it was before.

Over the pounding in her ears, she heard herself murmur, "I forbid it. You're not eighteen yet!"

She flounced to the cupboard, poured whiskey in a glass, added a little water and gulped it down. Her thoughts raced. Inconsiderate. Ungrateful. Selfish. She had sacrificed a lot to keep Penny in school. She should be willing to help out, now that she was graduated.

As she began to feel the calming warmth of the drink, she settled a smile on her face, lifted her chin and squared her shoulders.

"If you want to know the truth, I can't stand the thought of being a grandmother." She felt the tears sting her eyelids.

"Oh, Mom," Penny said, "don't worry about that. We don't plan to have a baby for at least four years."

"So, it's to be planned parenthood, huh?" Carla sneered.

"It has to be. You see, I'll be working while Ray is in seminary."

"Seminary? I thought he was studying to be a doctor. Seminaries are for preachers, aren't they?"

"Not just for preachers, Mom," Penny said. "Ray has just committed his life to the Lord's service. He knows he'll need more Bible training."

"And does that mean he's going to be a preacher?"

"He doesn't know yet." A hint of impatience sounded in Penny's voice. "He'll do what the Lord wants him to do."

"You mean he's willing to get married, but doesn't know how he'll support a wife?"

"Oh, Mom, you don't understand!"

"No, I *don't* understand. And don't try to brush me off with an answer like that!"

They ate breakfast in silence. Carla fumed inside. Penny was getting more like her father every day with that superior attitude that made Carla feel stupid.

"Mom, I'm sorry I upset you," Penny broke the silence. "I would like for you to understand how the Lord does lead people the way He wants them to go."

Carla winced. "I don't know why you're so religious lately. What's come over you?"

Penny jumped up and began to clear the table. A wall of silence seemed to rise between them.

Happy birthday to me, Carla thought. Aloud she said, "I've got to get the turkey on for company dinner tonight."

"Who's coming?"

"Grandmother, Aunt Irene and Uncle George is all."

"It's like Thanksgiving in June with a turkey, huh? Every day should be thanksgiving to God," she chirped.

Carla winced again.

By six o'clock, Penny's ecstatic chatter and constant activity were almost unbearable. Carla had gone to the cupboard for drink after drink all day. By the time George and Irene Grant arrived, her head was reeling. With a cup of black coffee in her hand, she met them at the door.

"Happy birthday, Sissy," they sang and kissed her cheek. "Mother didn't feel like coming. Another one of her migraines, she said." Irene dropped her purse on the floor, and put gift-wrapped packages on the coffee table.

"Do I smell turkey?" said George.

"You do," said Carla, "and that means we should all give thanks to God." She saw Penny look away.

After the meal, George leaned back and patted his flat stomach. "That's the best meal I've had since the last time we were here."

Irene laughed too loudly. "I wish I could cook. George says I should serve Rolaids for after-dinner mints." Everyone laughed.

Suddenly, Irene's attitude changed; the room became quiet. She sat slumped in her chair, her head lowered. Carla looked at George. He shook his head at her and turned to Penny. "Got another cup of coffee for your uncle?"

Before Penny could answer, Irene jumped up. "I'll get it," she said, and as she left the table, Carla caught a glimpse of a falling tear.

"What's wrong, George?" she whispered.

"That blasted town's getting her down." He glanced at Penny, then back at Carla. Penny took the hint and carried a stack of plates through the swinging doors to the kitchen.

"She's drinking too much," said George. "I don't know what's ahead for her if she doesn't get hold of herself. She wants to leave Idaho Springs, but Sis, I can't leave now." His eyes looked wild.

"Business is just beginning to boom. Tourist season is the only time I can make it. I've put a lot of money into repairs of the courts. I've got to get it back somehow." He sounded desperate. Carla touched his hand.

Just then Penny came through the door followed by Irene carrying the coffee pot. Carla stood and motioned to the living room. "Let's have it in there. More comfortable."

"Sorry I threw a wet blanket on the party." Irene flashed a smile, but her eyes were lusterless. She set the coffee pot on the

13

coffee table, then flopped on the couch, hugging a cushion. "I love this room, Sis. It's so elegant."

Carla turned on the lamps at each end of the table behind the couch, and rubbed her fingers along its rosewood surface. She loved nice things, too.

George lounged in one of the massive chairs, his legs stretched out in front of him. As Carla observed his rosy cheeks and round hazel eyes, his black, curly hair without a trace of gray, it was hard to believe he was thirty-seven. A lump came to her throat as she looked at Irene. She looked five years older than George.

"Are you working too hard at those tourist courts?"

"Who, me?" said Irene. "Of course not. You worry too much. What about you? You have to make it on your own."

A chill seemed to hover over them. Carla realized her problem was just as great as Irene's. Hadn't she been drinking all day? Then she leaned forward, remembering a happy thought.

"Do you know anyone who wants to buy a flourishing business and a fine suburban home? I'm leaving Englewood."

"Mom, when did you decide that? You didn't tell me about it." Penny stood next to Irene at the end of the couch.

"Is this a spur-of-the-moment idea?" asked George.

"Are you serious, Sis? What will you do with all your lovely things?" Irene looked distressed. "This is your home. Where will you go?"

Carla laughed out loud. "You'd think I said I'm going to die. That's what I've been doing. I want to live—now! I'm tired of the downhill plunge I've been taking."

She looked at Penny. "I didn't have a chance to tell you. You did most of the talking today, if you'll remember. George, do you think you can reserve a room for me in case I have to move before I decide what I want to do?"

"Be glad to have you and Penny near us, Sis."

"Not me and Penny," Carla said. "Maybe Penny would like to make her surprise announcement now."

"I wasn't going to say anything yet, Mom. I'm not sure if you approve."

"What difference would that make? You two have your minds made up."

"You're getting married!" Irene squealed. "I think it's wonderful, Kitten, if that's what you want." On the way to the kitchen, Irene said over her shoulder, "That calls for a drink."

A message passed between Carla and George. He shook his head and turned to Penny. "Set the date yet?"

"Probably around the first of August, if that's okay with Mom." Carla shrugged her shoulders and went to help Irene.

In the kitchen, Carla was surprised to see Irene tip the bottle of whiskey to her lips. She wondered how many she'd had already.

"This is a happy occasion in many ways," giggled Irene. "Your birthday, your decision to move, and now Penny . . ."

Carla helped carry the drinks to the living room.

"To Penny's happiness," said Irene, raising her glass. George and Carla joined in the toast. Penny looked shy and thanked them. "Now, how about your presents, Mom?"

"Oh, yes, Sissy. How about another toast to you?" Irene raised her glass again.

Then they sang "Happy Birthday" and sat down while Carla opened her packages. A gold compact, filmy lingerie, a bracelet—just the kind of things she liked. Then, there was a book. Carla would never select a book for anyone. It was from her mother and the title of it seemed to point a finger of disapproval at her.

Keep Your Thinking Right, she laughed as she read it. Opening the book to the first page, she continued, "Life is what you make it. Keep your thinking right and your life will be right." She closed the book and tossed it on the coffee table.

"There's your answer," she said. "Just think it and it's so."

Before she realized what was happening, Penny had dropped to the floor at Carla's knees. "Mom," her voice was high-pitched. "Mom, that isn't the answer," she blurted. "I know where to find the real answers . . ." Carla was shocked by Penny's rudeness, but she went on in a kind of life or death attitude.

"Remember when I told you I made a decision for Christ?" The room was cathedral-quiet. All eyes were fixed on Penny. "I went forward in church—the church Ray and his folks go to . . ."

Carla jiggled her foot up and down. She was irritated and embarrassed. George looked amused. Irene seemed extremely interested.

"Do you think this is the time for a sermon?" Carla asked sarcastically.

"Please listen, Mom. It's important. I know you're all mixed up." Tears spilled from her eyes.

"Let her talk, Sis," Irene insisted. "I think we're all mixed up. Go on, Kitten, tell us what you learned in church."

Carla's attention was held by Penny's fixed gaze. "I learned that Jesus Christ is the answer to all our problems. All you have to do is ask Him to come into your life."

She reached out and touched Carla's arm. "Mom, won't you ask Him to come in? Please, Mom."

"Don't be ridiculous!" Carla pushed her hand away. Penny jumped up and ran down the hall.

Had she been too blunt with the girl? Why would Penny try to put her on the spot like that? She had a right to live her own life!

Before she had time to wonder further, Penny was back. She placed a Bible in Carla's hand.

"Here, Mom. You'll find the answers you need in this Book."

"What's going on here?" Carla held the Book with her thumb and forefinger. "Here, take it. You and your grandmother both know I never read. Put it on my nightstand. I might take a look at it when I have more time." She waved her hand before her face, dismissing it from her mind.

George got up, thrust his hands in his hip pockets, and strolled about the room.

"Where do you think you'll go, eventually?" he asked, standing in front of her.

"Hell, no doubt—according to Penny." She got up, poured a drink, then moved to her desk.

"Heard from Rich Preston the other day. He still wants us to come to California and live with them. To force the issue, he sent this." She watched George's expression as he looked at the snapshot.

"Wow! What a house! Do they still live in Beverly Hills?"

"I knew you'd be impressed," Carla laughed. "Yes, they're still in Beverly Hills. I wish I knew what he does for a living." She put the picture back in the desk drawer. She didn't see Penny standing in the hall doorway.

16

"I sort of remember him," Penny said. "I saw him once when I was real little, and then again at Daddy's funeral. He looked like a real grandfather with all that white hair."

Carla went on to explain to George, "Herb never knew his father until he came to see us when Penny was about four years old. He deserted Herb's mother before Herb was born."

"How did he act toward Herb?" asked George.

Carla was interrupted by Irene's impatient whine. "It's time to go home now, Sis. Come on, George. You know how mother hates to be alone up there in that wicked town."

"It is late," said Carla. "How can I thank you for helping me celebrate my birthday? Thank mother for the book, too. It may be just what I need."

She closed and locked the door, then looked at Penny. Neither spoke. Carla thought of the nightmare. The same longing and empty hopelessness seemed to possess her now. What did she want? What was she seeking? Was there such a thing as real happiness?

2

Carla Preston propped two pillows behind her back, turned on the reading lamp beside her bed and picked up the book from her mother.

"Keep Your Thinking Right." Was that the answer? Her lip curled in skepticism. Before she could open the book, the phone rang. No one but Jim called after ten.

"Happy birthday, honey." The low, southern drawl brought a mental picture of the tall, lanky young man with tousled blond hair, sensitive mouth and sleepy blue eyes.

"Jim, darling, you remembered. Where are you?"

"At The Hideaway. Can I come and get you?"

"I'm sorry, darling. I'd love to see you, but not tonight. Had a big day with the family, you know."

His soft love words crooned in her ear and ended with the inevitable question, "Do you love me, honey?"

"You know I do," she whispered. "We'll get together tomorrow. Goodnight, darling."

Putting the phone back in its cradle, she thought of her decision to leave Englewood. Letting Jim go would be the first and most difficult step she must take to regain her self-respect.

Again, she propped herself up and reached for the book. Carla smiled at the first chapter heading, "Love Everyone." That shouldn't be too hard, especially if there were more people like Jim Frazer. But—love *everyone?* Mr. Barker, too? She shuddered at the thought.

Reading the next chapter heading, Carla was startled by the harshness of her own laughter. "Let Your Mind Dwell on Good Things." *That* called for a drink. She rolled out of bed and stalked down the hall, pushing light switches on her way to the kitchen.

On the way back to bed with a tall drink in her hand, she almost ran into Penny framed in the doorway, her face white and eyes wide.

"I thought I heard something. You okay, Mom?"

"Of course." Carla felt irritated. "Just couldn't sleep. This ought to help." She lifted her glass in a toast-gesture and flipped past Penny, her nose in the air.

Back in bed, she balanced her drink in one hand and the book in the other. She read the heading once more. "Let Your Mind Dwell on Good Things." Like what? A goody-goody daughter? Fortieth birthday? Or, maybe she should let her mind dwell on things like alcoholism, lung cancer, and nightmares!

Drowsy, but afraid to go to sleep for fear of a return engagement of the nightmare, she got up and paced the floor. If she could only stop thinking. Another drink?

Tiptoeing down the hall, she was determined to be quiet. Penny mustn't hear her this time. She closed the kitchen door before switching on the light. She poured a drink, and after careful consideration, came to the conclusion that it would be much safer to do all her drinking right there in the kitchen. She gulped the whiskey down and stared at the empty glass—would that do it? Had to be sure. She splashed two more jiggers in the glass, a little water—very little. Down the hatch.

As she started toward the door, the walls began to move. Faster and faster they turned. It took all her strength to push open the swinging doors. By this time the floor was spinning counter-clockwise to the walls. She saw herself floating, her arms and legs floundering above the floor. The dining room carpet reached for her face.

Consciousness struggled with a dull headache. A smile played at the corners of Carla Preston's mouth as, through half-closed eyes, she saw dancing sunbeams sifting through filmy, white curtains and falling across the bedspread.

A search through scattered pictures in her mind revealed nothing of the horrible nightmare. What a relief! But—was this the answer? To stop the nightmare, was every evening to end in an alcoholic blackout? She groaned. What about those good resolutions? In spite of the effort to control herself, convulsive sobs rocked her body. How could she face Penny? No one else could have helped her back to bed.

With concentrated attention, she struggled through a cold shower. In a short time, skin tingling and mind somewhat cleared,

Carla was ready to face the new day—and Penny.

Breezing into the kitchen, she dropped a slice of bread in the toaster and poured a cup of coffee. One hand on her hip, she said, "Sorry about last night, Kitten."

The open Bible in front of Penny seemed to point a finger of guilt at Carla. She searched her daughter's face for understanding, but received nothing but a shiny, blue-eyed stare.

"I guess I had too much to drink—all day and evening. After I went to bed, I couldn't sleep. That's when you saw me with a drink—" Was that a twitch of humor at the corner of Penny's mouth? "Still couldn't sleep—but you didn't hear me that time—did you?"

Penny's shoulders were shaking. The wall was down, for the moment, at least.

"Anyway, thanks a lot for helping me out. I won't ask for details. It must have been scary for you."

Later, on her way out Carla said, "Why don't you call Aunt Irene today and ask if she'll help with your bridesmaids' dresses? And while you have her on the phone, ask her to reserve rooms for Jim Frazer and Cecil Barker for the night of July third." She threw a kiss and stepped out the door.

At her little Exotic Gifts Shop, Carla greeted clerks in adjoining concessions, unlocked her cash register and inspected shelves and counters. A lump arose in her throat as she picked up a feather duster. She had put a lot of herself into this little business. It had been a kind of proving ground—proof of her capabilities, independence and self-assurance.

She still remembered the time she had told Herb Preston she wanted a divorce. His positive, caustic remark, "You can't get along without me," had left her totally defeated.

Well, she had proven—at least to herself—that she could get along without anyone. She felt secure in the midst of all these exotic pieces. Her fingers caressed the outlines of a bronze Grecian figure. She lifted the top of an ornately carved ivory music box, and smiled at the simple melody. Her eyes swept across the rows of uniquely designed wall clocks with their many moving parts. Her stock was valuable. Every cent was tied up in this shop and her house. Her savings was almost nil.

The morning wore on. Business was brisk for such a hot day. "Cool Colorado" registered ninety degrees before noon. Wiping her face with a tissue, she finished giftwrapping one of her favorite antique bracelets. She rang up the sale on the antique cash register, a prized possession, and before she turned around, she felt his presence.

Jim Frazer lounged over the counter, unveiled love in his sleepy, blue eyes. Carla glanced about the shop. Most of her customers knew Jim and his wife, Sue. If he didn't try to hide their relationship, why should she?

Elbows on the counter, her face close to his, she whispered, "It's been a long time, darling."

His lips brushed her hair. "Lunch together?"

"Same place?" she asked.

"Uh-huh. Twelve-thirty." Hands thrust in hip pockets, dreamy-eyed, he strolled out. Her eyes followed him. *Could* she let him go?

The morning dragged on. At last it was time for lunch. Carla's heart skipped across her breast as she came to the end of the winding, tree-bordered lane. The Hideaway, a little tavern nestled in the foothills, was their favorite meeting place. Tall lilac hedges, like sentinels, guarded the small, vine-covered building and graveled parking area.

She stepped from her car and pretended surprise as Jim's long arm darted from behind a giant shrub and folded her to his chest. She looked into the depths of his eyes. Then, nothing else mattered but the pressure of his soft lips on hers.

Like truant school children, they ran down the graveled parking lot into the dim refuge of The Hideaway. Inside, she stood still to let her eyes adjust to the dim candlelight.

They went to their special corner. Holding hands across the table, their eyes locked, Jim whispered, "I've missed you, honey."

Her throaty laugh teased him. "How many years has it been?"

"Be serious. I've got something important to tell you. Last night after I talked to you, I went right home. It wasn't late, but Sue was so mad at me she told me to leave and never come back. That's the first time she's ever said that. I don't know what brought it on. Probably some nosy neighbor told her something. What does

21

that sound like to you? Do you think she might be thinking about getting a divorce?"

His words tumbled over each other in his excitement. Carla felt the blood drain from her heart. How many times Jim had said he wanted to marry her if Sue ever divorced him. Carla had considered it such a remote possibility she had never taken him seriously. But now he sounded very serious.

Did she *really* want to marry Jim? He was much younger than she, and not too ambitious—but he was romantic. Could this be the solution for her decision to regain her self-respect?

"Well, what are you gonna say, hon? You don't look too happy. You do love me, don't you?"

"Of course, Jim darling. I'm happy."

He sighed and leaned back, a boyish grin on his face. " I want you to listen to this." He dug a slip of paper from his shirt pocket. "I wrote it last night, just for you."

In the intimacy of the high-walled booth, his soft, Southern accent crooned his latest love song, "Come, let me hold you, come, hold me again."

She listened to all the verses. "It's beautiful, Jim. Did you really write it just for me?"

He folded the paper and put it back in his pocket, slipped out of the booth and slid to her side. He held her face in his hands, and after a lingering kiss, he said, "That's my answer, sweet Carla."

Later, in her car, it was difficult to leave Jim. He seemed to cling to her for assurance. Closing the door and leaning inside for a last kiss, he asked, "When will I see you again?"

"Oh, Jim, I almost forgot to tell you. I'm going to Idaho Springs for the week of the fourth. Of course, we'll see each other in the meantime, but listen to this. George wants you to sing up there on the night of the third. It's their annual Gold Rush Days send-off. I've already reserved a room for you at their motel."

His boyish face brightened. "You're pretty sure of yourself, aren't you? What time do you want me to pick you up on the third?"

Carla hesitated. She didn't know how he'd take this.

"Jim, darling. Mr. Barker asked to take me up a long time ago."

"I don't like that!" Jim grabbed her wrist. "You're my woman."

Carla patted his hand. "It'll be okay. You and I will be together a lot," she promised.

"I still don't like it. You're mine, and only mine!"

"Not yet. I can still hear the chains jangling." She laughed and waved goodbye. "Call me tonight, darling."

The following week was a strain on Carla, mentally and physically. Her house was being shown every day, which meant a daily cleaning. Penny's wedding plans were under way and Penny sometimes needed her advice and supervision. She had to break in a woman to manage her shop for a week. Jim was more demanding of her time, exhibiting a nervous insecurity. Then, to ward off the persistent nightmare, she'd sneak to the kitchen every night after Penny was in bed for drink after drink.

When would she be out of this maze? The week in Idaho Springs might help. As for pursuing the idea of regaining her self-respect, she'd give it up until she sold her house and business and left this small town of Englewood for good. And left Jim, too.

On the afternoon of July third, Carla waved to Cecil Barker from the picture window as the shiny black Lincoln Continental stopped in front of her house. She took a quick mental check of all safety precautions: locked windows and doors, disconnected television, automatic night light, refrigerator on vacation dial. Satisfied, she picked up her overnight case and, with her foot, pushed the heavy traveling bag out the front door. Mr. Barker was there, waiting for her. It always amazed Carla that a man that size could move so fast.

As they drove away, Carla looked back at the modest little brick bungalow located on the shady, quiet street, and wondered why there were no happy memories there.

"You look lovely, as usual, Carla, my dear." Cecil Barker interrupted her thoughts. She saw his beady eyes slide over her, and felt her face flush.

Looking at him, squeezed behind the wheel—no waist, no neck, and apparently no joints—he reminded her of a huge balloon. She shivered involuntarily at the sight of his small hands on the steering wheel and his tiny feet in their highly-polished shoes. But, she remembered he was a big spender, a powerful figure in the community, and she was sure he wouldn't make advances toward her.

At least she hoped not. The back of her neck prickled at the thought of being alone with him for the next hour and a half. She'd been with him on many occasions, but always in the company of at least two or three other women. He was noted for surrounding himself with beautiful women.

Come to think of it—she really didn't know him well at all. Still called him Mr. Barker. He wasn't the kind of person you ever felt you knew well enough to call by his first name.

At the first intersection, Carla was aware of a small, dark green car following them. She pulled down the sun visor and looked in the mirror. The car seemed to be keeping a set pace behind them. After several blocks, she said, "Are we being followed, Mr. Barker?"

His small eyes darted to the rear view mirror. "My bodyguards," he wheezed. "They're getting a little careless."

Fear clouded Carla's vision, blurring the features of the men in the car behind them. Mr. Barker offered no explanation. She flipped the visor back in position and brushed the incident from her mind. This was her vacation. She intended to make the most of it. She'd give no further thought to the mysterious bodyguards or Mr. Barker's suggestive glances.

She loved the drive to Idaho Springs, first through the rolling, green foothills, then through the red boulders, streams, and pines as the road became steeper and more winding. She rested her head on the headrest; her body sank into the soft leather upholstery. The luxury of Mr. Barker's Lincoln Continental dispelled her anxieties and fears for the moment.

On the outskirts of Idaho Springs, Mr. Barker made an unexpected turn off the highway. Driving down a shady side street, he came to a slow stop under a tall pine tree. The area was unoccupied except for a few abandoned houses, windows broken and boarded, fences down and yards overgrown with weeds.

Mr. Barker switched off the ignition, and touched a button, letting all the windows down. He shifted his heavy bulk toward Carla and heaved his jointless arm to the back of the seat behind her head.

Carla had never been afraid of Mr. Barker, but her earlier uneasiness returned.

"Carla, my dear," he wheezed in a chronic, asthmatic voice, "I'd like to talk seriously with you about something I've had on my mind a long time."

The meaning of his words was lost in Carla's concentration on the long strand of hair combed so carefully over the top of his head, which was completely bald, except for some gray fringe over his collar. Lowering her eyes, she shuddered at the enormous bulk inside the expensive gray suit.

"Whatever is wrong with you, Mr. Barker?" His words finally penetrated her understanding.

"There's never been anything serious between us." She forced a ripple of laughter, which was quickly followed by a chill at the sight of the quick, lifeless smile that twitched his upper lip.

"Then, I think it's about time, my dear." He took a spotless handkerchief from his hip pocket, wiped his forehead, and folded and replaced it.

"I'd like to offer you a business proposition. It isn't an impossible task, and I don't expect your answer right now." He shifted his weight back to the front, put his hands on the steering wheel and looked straight ahead.

"I need a business companion—a woman like you. Intelligent, beautiful—" his voice was a monotone. "She must be willing to live where I live. I do travel a lot. There will be light secretarial work, and I need a charming hostess for my social affairs, and a delightful companion when I must go out." His eyes darted in her direction. "One last thing—you'll never want for anything as long as you live."

Without giving her an opportunity to answer one way or the other, the powerful motor roared and tires crunched the gravel as he headed for Grant's Haven where, not more than six blocks away, they came to a noiseless stop at the manager's office.

George rushed out to open the door, a smile on his ruddy face.

"You got here early. It's good to see you, Sis. This must be Mr. Cecil Barker. I'll show you to your room, Sir."

"That'll be fine, young man. The little lady can use help, too, especially with the big box."

25

"It's my costume, George. You'll love it."

Carla took her overnight case from the front seat and called over her shoulder, "See you tonight, Mr. Barker."

Irene met her at the door of the manager's quarters. She clung to Carla a moment, then guided her down the hall to the back bedroom.

"Mother wants you to use her room 'til she gets back. She went to her friend's for the weekend—said she couldn't take all the commotion here. You can have one of the courts after that if you like, or you can sleep on the couch here."

Carla laughed and threw herself on the bed.

"Here, at last. Let me relax and forget everything for a while. I've got so much to tell you, Irene."

She kicked off her shoes and tucked her feet under her. "My house is sold. Got the price I asked, too. Penny's hilarious about getting married and leaving me. Just think how free I'll be. And, what do you think about this? Jim's wife will probably get a divorce and he's dying to marry me—and, listen to this—just a few minutes ago, I received a *fabulous* offer from Mr. Barker." She threw back her head and laughed.

Irene giggled. "What's so funny about the offer? What did he say?"

Just a simple little offer, like wanting me to live with him and be his very own private secretary, his very own private hostess, his very own private companion."

"And what little token does he give for those little services?" laughed Irene.

Carla turned over on her stomach, her head resting on her arms. "For those little chores, he'll see to it that I never want for anything as long as I live."

"That's not a bad offer, Sis. Isn't he very wealthy?"

Was Irene serious?

"No, not bad at all," Carla sounded bitter. "Yes, he's wealthy, all right. A rambling ranchhouse, several hotels, a cattle ranch, a wheat farm. And the minor items like: a Lincoln Continental, a three carat diamond stick pin, a thousand dollar bill he flaunts everywhere he goes—but, there's *Cecil Barker* included in the package."

Carla's ears began to roar, her voice choked with anger. "I know I'm not getting any younger, but I still have a few principles left—and a dream or two."

"Talk about dreams—Jim's in room seven. Wants to know the minute you get here. What are you planning to do about him, Sis?"

Carla jumped up, stepped into her shoes, took a quick look in the mirror, and smiled.

"I don't know yet. I'll go find out."

3

Across the patio, beneath the grape arbor, and through the side entrance of the tourist lodge Carla Preston ran. She stopped a moment for breath before tapping her finger tips on the door of room seven. The tall, blond country singer drew her in and shut the door.

"Alone at last," he whispered in her hair.

She melted in his embrace, lost in the sensation of deep waters rolling over her head. Then, she felt herself being lifted in his arms and carried across the room.

A sudden knock at the door broke the spell of their stolen moment. Before she knew what was happening, she found herself closed in a small, dark closet. Jim's words came from the other side. "I'll get rid of 'em as fast as I can, honey."

Carla held her breath and listened. Her anxieties faded for the moment as her cheek brushed the satin smoothness of one of Jim's jewelled western jackets. Her senses reeled with the familiar fragrance of Old Spice.

Muffled words came through the door. "Pardon me, young man, could I borrow some ice?" That asthmatic wheeze made Carla shiver. Was Mr. Barker suspicious of her and Jim?

"Say, aren't you that country singer?"

"I sing country songs, yes. I don't think I know you," Jim drawled.

"Name's Barker. Cecil Barker."

After a short pause, Carla heard Jim's voice crack. "Oh, yes, I believe I have heard of you."

"Thanks for the ice. Care to join me in a drink?"

"We'll have to make it later, Mr. Barker. I'm due to sing at the hotel in about an hour."

"Fine, fine. I'll see you there. What's your name again?"

"Jim Frazer."

When Carla heard the door close, she ran out and threw her arms around Jim's neck. "Oh, Jim, I can't go on like this. I feel so cheap."

He held her head to his chest. "I'm sorry, honey. I promise you it won't be long now. When I'm free . . ."

She put her fingers on his lips, pulled his head down and kissed him. Looking both ways down the corridor, she brushed past him and ran out the door.

Outside, she took a deep breath of fresh mountain air. If only her life could be cleansed, too! She *must* tell Jim they were through.

An hour later, the humiliating experience was crowded from her mind as Carla entered the world of seductive splendor known as the Gold Rush Days.

She stepped from Mr. Barker's long, black Lincoln Continental and made a vibrant entrance into the plush hotel lobby. Her costume, an exact copy of a Lillian Russell original, enhanced her natural beauty and restored her self-respect, for the moment at least. Its royal-blue taffeta molded her tiny hourglass figure from the bust line to her knees, then billowed to the tops of high-buttoned shoes. A large, ostrich-plumed hat framed her tilt-nose profile.

She flipped a backward glance at Cecil Barker and was pleased with his portrayal of Diamond Jim. Along with a full-dress suit and tall, silk top hat, she saw that he had added his own touch of authenticity. A genuine three-carat diamond stick pin nestled in his black silk cravat. But the most recognizable characteristic of Diamond Jim was the three hundred pounds of flesh Mr. Barker carried.

As they passed through the lobby, without warning Carla's attention was captured by eyes that seemed to sparkle their own private appraisal, and an amused smile that seemed to flash his approval. The fleeting signal between them was, just as suddenly, disconnected. Mr. Barker stepped to her side, completely blocking her view of the stranger.

Irene and George Grant met them at the dining hall entrance. As a member of the Chamber of Commerce, George was assigned the role of host, with Irene as hostess, for the evening.

"Wow! You're a knock-out, Sis." George bowed over her hand. "Come, I'll show you to your table."

"Wait a minute, George. I want to show her the decorations," interrupted Irene. "Will you excuse us, Mr. Barker?"

29

"Everything is simply beautiful," exclaimed Carla. "Where in the world did you get the lamps?"

On every table an antique, hand-painted oil lamp cast a rosy glow on white damask cloths. Beside each lamp lay a single rose bud that seemed to offer romance for the evening.

"We got them from the natives—some from the Teller House, some from Alpine Lodge, others from our own neighbors."

Irene led her away from Mr. Barker.

"I wanted to tell you something, Sis. Jim said a strange thing to me earlier when he came in. I don't know if he'd been drinking or not, but anyway, he said, 'Irene, how'd you like to have a brother-in-law? It won't be long, now.' Are you going to marry him?"

"No, I'm not!" Carla was indignant.

Coming back to their table, Carla was surprised at the animated conversation between Mr. Barker and George. How could those two have anything in common?

They both got to their feet and pulled chairs out for the ladies. Irene shook her head and put her arm through George's. "Let's go to the bar for a quick one," she said. "You two be good now. Would you like for us to order something for you, Mr. Barker?"

"Yes, that'll be fine. Two martinis, and send me your tab."

Why did they have to leave her alone with Mr. Barker? Irene didn't need a drink right now. She'd probably get loud and weepy before the evening was over.

As soon as they were out of sight, Mr. Barker covered her hand with his. "Have you been thinking over our conversation, my dear?"

"Not really," Carla forced a smile and drew her hand away.

Resting her chin in her hands, her eyes swept over the crowd. From the corner of her eye she saw Mr. Barker open his wallet before the waitress. She knew he was going to flash that thousand dollar bill again, and watch the waitress' startled expression through half-closed eyes. Was it a quirk with him? He had put on that little performance at least once during every evening she had been with him. That might be the reason for bodyguards, she mused.

Music started. The program was about to begin. It featured

some of the local talent, but Jim was the headline singer. As people returned to their tables, Carla realized she couldn't see the platform from where she was sitting. She had promised Jim she'd be watching. She glanced at Mr. Barker, then slipped out of her chair, patted his shoulder and smiled. "Please excuse me a minute. And don't drink my drink."

She made her way through the crowded tables, trying to reach a space by the wall opposite the platform. She concentrated on the floor because it was difficult to manage her full skirt through the narrow places.

When she did look up, her eyes met those of the handsome stranger. There was that same twinkle of amusement! As she stood looking at him, he leaped up and was beside her in an instant.

He tucked her hand under his arm and strolled back to his table. "What kept you so long?" He pulled out a chair.

"How long have you been waiting?" she laughed.

"All my life."

"And where did you do all this waiting?"

"Everywhere—parks, beaches, planes, north, south, east, west."

The chanting of her heart drowned out the strains of a popular love song sung by a young girl country singer. She felt weak as she sat down in the chair he held for her. Her eyes followed him as he moved to the chair opposite her.

When he reached for her hands in the rosy glow of the lamp, Carla knew this was her dream of romance.

Suddenly the twinkle of mischief was there again. "I wonder how you'd look in faded jeans and sneakers?"

She threw back her head and laughed. "In this setting?" She leaned forward. "They'd be a lot more comfortable," she whispered.

He turned her hand over and touched the dinner ring on her left hand. "Not taken," he mused.

At that moment, Jim Frazer bent over the table. "How did you like it? My new song—you know, honey, the one I wrote for you. How did you like it?" He talked fast.

Carla felt the blood drain from her face. She hadn't even

listened to his song.

"Jim, darling," she stammered, "I'd like you to meet . . ." She didn't even know the name of the man who still held her hands.

"The man" rose and shook Jim's hand. "Marc Randall. How are you, Jim?"

Jim looked blank. "Do I know you? How do you know me?"

"Your picture is in the foyer, and I've heard you sing before. I think it was with a western group up in Georgetown about a year ago."

"Oh, yeah, I was up there once. I gotta get back now." He frowned at Carla, turned on his heel and walked away. As he disappeared in the crowd, Carla wondered why he suddenly looked so boyish.

Then everything else was forgotten. Marc lifted her hands to his lips, and looking from under dark eyebrows, asked, "Carla what?"

Her breath caught in her throat; she felt the blood rise to her forehead. Her big hat seemed to weigh her head down. When she did find her voice, words tumbled out.

"Carla Preston. My husband died five years ago. I have a teenage daughter, Penny. She's getting married next month."

Why did she want to tell him everything? Was it the way he looked into the depths of her eyes as if she were the most important person in his life?

"I'm visiting my sister," she went on. "Just sold my house in Englewood. My little gift shop is up for sale."

She paused for breath, then sighed, "I really don't know much about the future."

A smile crinkled the corners of his mouth. "How about the present?"

She closed her eyes, then looked directly into his. "It looks good," she smiled.

Suddenly his hands tightened on hers. She followed his gaze across the room. Cecil Barker sat facing them, his short arms across his chest.

"I do believe he's angry," said Carla.

"What is he to you?" The bluntness of Marc's question startled her. Her chest tightened.

"He's a very good friend of mine," she said, cooly.

Marc stood and offered her his arm. As they started across the room, he bent over and in a soft, yet emphatic, tone whispered, "I must see you again."

Kaleidoscopic pictures passed before her eyes, memories of her past weaknesses. She was afraid to see him again. He was too attractive, too interesting, too self-assured . . .

"I'm staying at my sister's house. Her husband is the owner of Grant's Tourist Haven." She was too weak to say no.

Marc led her to Mr. Barker's table, and after he helped her to her chair, he faced the big man. "My apologies for monopolizing Miss Lillian Russell."

Cecil Barker ignored Marc, labored to his feet and, from behind Carla's chair, whispered in her ear. "Your presence is all I've required, so far."

Marc lifted her hand from the table and held it to his lips. " 'Til tomorrow at ten, my lady," he smiled.

As she watched his figure move through the crowded tables, her thoughts raced. Could this be the beginning of her dream of self-respect, or was it just another shadow walking out of her life?

Mr. Barker brought her out of her reverie and back to a very real present. Wooden-faced, he lifted her to her feet and, like an angry father, hustled her out of the dining room through the lobby and out to the car.

Carla, stunned beyond protest, sat on the edge of the seat and stared out the window. The big car roared down the tree-lined street and made a sharp curve onto the Virginia Canyon road that led to Central City.

Tears of anger and humiliation stung her eyes. "Will you kindly tell me where you are taking me?"

His deadly-soft answer multiplied her fears. "Relax. you'll find out."

She slid back in her seat, her hands clasped in her lap. The back of her head and neck ached. It must be the heavy hat. She pulled out the long hat pin and placed the hat on the seat between them. What an ideal weapon! Slowly, with her eyes on Mr. Barker, Carla worked it into the folds of her skirt.

The heavy-jowled profile was barely discernable in the misty

33

light of a waning moon. Even though Carla did not know Mr. Barker well, she had not thought him capable of such subterfuge. He had now become a complete stranger to her. She couldn't believe what was happening. It was just like an old-fashioned melodrama. High-strung, nerves on edge, Carla began to laugh hysterically. Mr. Barker's small hand shot out and clutched her arm with a sharp, sobering pain.

"This is no laughing matter," he hissed. "Don't think you're getting away with your little performance. I'm nobody's fool. Oh, I let you think I was, as long as you didn't humiliate me. But tonight you really went too far."

Carla's face felt feverish. Hearing the truth about herself once again shattered her hopes of regaining her self-respect.

"I'm sorry, Mr. Barker. Truly I am. Now, won't you please take me back to my sister's?"

A sudden lurch of speed and recklessness was his answer. Carla shut her eyes and held her hands over her ears, but the screeching tires on hairpin curves could still be heard. Minutes seemed like agonizing hours before the car came to a stop.

Every tense muscle in her body ached as she slid out of the car. The summer theater crowd streamed down the main street. She wanted to cry for help; instead, she squared her shoulders, lifted her chin and touched the hat pin, still tucked in the folds of her dress. She could take care of herself.

With a pretense of courage, Carla kept pace with Mr. Barker, who literally ploughed his way through the crowds and into the new Silverton Inn. Society's cream of the crop filled the lobby, waiting to be seated in the luxurious dining room.

Carla caught a glimpse of herself in a huge mirror that covered one complete wall. She looked out of place in her crumpled Lillian Russell costume—hair disheveled, face pale, lipstick gone. The other ladies were tall and slender, elegantly groomed in their latest formal gowns. Mr. Barker had no right to put her in a situation like this. She must get away from him.

He evidently saw her eyes dart toward the desk phone. His small hand closed on her arm.

"Come, my dear." He crowded her into a small elevator, pressed the button, and wheezed on her neck. In the airless cage, she felt suspended in a vacuum. Something had to be done. But what?

The elevator doors slid open; her feet sank into the deep pile carpeting of a small entrance hall. Her palms were icy-damp; a rubber band seemed to be tightening around her throat.

Mr. Barker opened an elaborately carved door into a luxury apartment. The moment the door closed his manner seemed to change from menacing evil to gracious hospitality.

He led her to a low, leather-upholstered couch, placed a large, soft cushion at her back, then lumbered to the fireplace and lit the logs.

"It gets cool up here, even in July." He stood with his back to the fireplace and watched her under folded eyelids. After an interval of silence, he said, "I want you to relax. I'll be back shortly."

What an order! Did he say relax? In the midst of imminent danger?

When Mr. Barker returned, he had changed from his Diamond Jim Brady costume into casual lounging attire. Carla was fascinated by the unique design on the pocket of his smoking jacket. Richly embroidered in gold and white silk, and embellished by a single deep-red ruby, it was too intricately woven to decipher.

The big man lowered his weight into a large club chair, selected a pipe from a rack on the end-table next to it, and took a velvet bag from a small drawer. Methodically he filled the pipe, packed down the tobacco, and finally lit it. After taking several short puffs to get it started, he leaned back and heaved a sigh.

"You see, my dear," he wheezed from behind a cloud of smoke, "I can be quite domestic."

Carla shuddered, squirmed to a more comfortable position, and pretended to be occupied with the contents of her purse.

"What do you think of my latest enterprise?" he asked. "I've just purchased the Silverton Inn."

His voice rose to a higher pitch. Carla couldn't remember ever having heard enthusiasm in his voice before.

"Now that many of the old historical buildings are being restored, Central City will be one of the state's biggest tourist attractions, especially with the increased interest in the opera. I foresee a boom in business here."

He seemed to wait for her to speak. She raised her eyes slowly, deliberately void of expression. "The only thing that is of interest to me, Mr. Barker, is your immediate plans for me!"

4

Mr. Barker coughed, laid down his pipe, and struggled to his feet. "You do come to the point, don't you, my dear?"

She felt the couch sag as he eased down beside her. "If you want direct answers, I'll give them to you."

Carla Preston stiffened her back, and folded her arms across her breast as he reached for her hand.

"Don't be afraid, my dear. I won't harm you, but I'll admit I was a little upset for a time." His voice drummed on while Carla listened with mindless intensity—her only thought, to escape.

"After observing your beauty and charm tonight, I realized I wanted you more than anything else in the world. Then, to see a perfect stranger take you away was more than I could bear. I lost control of myself for a time."

"You abducted me. You're holding me now against my will." She felt a surge of courage. "I can't forgive you for that."

He heaved closer to her. "What I'm trying to say, Carla—will you marry me?"

Nausea dimmed her vision. What would he do if she refused? Her hand slipped down the folds of her dress and touched the hat pin. Sliding to the edge of the couch, she rose to her full height and inched toward the door. With a boldness she didn't feel, she forced a smile and cooed, "It's absolutely unthinkable."

She turned on her heel and started for the door. Mr. Barker raced to the door. His hurtling mass caught Carla by surprise. Her lungs filled with air she was unable to expel. A purple-faced, enraged Cecil Barker blocked the only way out.

A dull ache, which started at her fingertips, made its way to her heart and numbed her mind. Smitten with sudden loneliness for Penny, Carla wished she knew how to pray.

At the sound of the door chimes, the huge man wheeled around, wild-eyed, and flung himself, spread-eagle, against the door. Had Mr. Barker's mind snapped?

"Who is it?" she screamed, gasping for breath.

"George. Is that you, Carla?"

Cecil Barker seemed to deflate before her eyes. He turned and looked at her. Before he opened the door, he wheezed, "You win this time."

George Grant bounded to Carla's side.

"I'm sorry, Mr. Barker, but my wife needs Carla right away." He whisked her to the door.

In the safety of George's car, Carla began to shake. "You came just in time," she quavered.

"You must have had a rough time, Sis. I saw you leave with him. He looked mad as a hornet."

"He was—said I was using him."

"Well, I'm glad you're okay. Why did he take you to his apartment?"

"Believe it or not, he wanted to ask me to marry him."

"Wow, you could do a lot worse."

"Oh, George, you make me so mad. Money isn't everything."

"Have it your way," he grinned and started the car. "I'm glad you refused, Sis."

"I'm afraid Mr. Barker didn't take no for an answer. By the way, how did you know where to find me?"

"Mr. Barker made a point of telling me of his new enterprise, the Silverton Inn. I had an idea he wanted you to see it."

Carla leaned her head against the seat and closed her eyes. She had learned a sure way to forget unpleasant things was to think of something pleasant.

Marc Randall! Twinkling eyes, amused smile, deep resonant voice! Her thoughts were fully occupied the rest of the way home.

Irene was asleep when they came in.

Carla said, "So—she didn't really need me after all."

"Nope—just too much to drink, as usual."

"Well, thanks anyway for being in the right place at the right time. Goodnight now."

The next morning, a rested and refreshed Carla breezed into the kitchen. Irene was in bathrobe and slippers, completely out of harmony with the bright, sun-drenched kitchen. She mumbled something under her breath, poured two cups of coffee, and motioned Carla to sit down.

"My head's splitting. You look sober. I don't know how you do it. Tell me about the handsome guy you were mooning over."

"There's nothing to tell." Why did she have to blush?

"Who is he? Are you going to see him again?"

"His name's Marc Randall, and yes, I am going to see him again—in exactly two minutes. I don't know where we're going or what we'll do, but whatever it is—I'm ready."

At the sound of the door bell, she raced down the hall, grabbed her shoulder bag, and called through the kitchen door, "I'll be back by two. Promised to see Jim before he goes home. I think I'll forget him—for today, at least."

She threw open the door. There he stood—at the bottom of the steps. Firecrackers in the next yard popped with the same excitement she felt in her breast.

Holding her at arm's length, light dancing in his eyes and amusement crinkling his mouth, he said, "Complete down to sneakers." With her hand in his, they ran to the low, green convertible at the curb.

"I'm mixing business with pleasure today. Hope you don't mind."

The powerful sports car roared around a sharp curve and onto the Virginia Canyon road.

For a second, the memory of the wild ride with Cecil Barker the night before cast a shadow on her happiness. Dismissing the memory, she asked, "What is your business, Mr. Marc Randall?"

"I'm glad you remembered my name. I'm an insurance investigator—with a firm in Los Angeles—on a case up here."

"Sounds exciting."

"Not half as exciting as being with you. Now, Carla Preston, tell me—what are some of your interests?"

Her breath caught in her throat. Her answer to that particular question had always been, "Men, what else?" She groped for a better answer.

"I really don't know. My interests are limited. You might say I've been on an ego-trip since my husband died, but I've made up my mind to change all that."

"How do you plan to go about it?"

"I haven't the faintest idea," she sighed.

Marc took his foot off the accelerator and swung into a parking area constructed for the convenience of sightseers. He pulled her out on his side of the car, and still holding her hand, strolled to a stone wall overlooking the canyon.

The sun was high, but a cool breeze whispered through the tall pines. He lifted her hands and held them against his chest, drawing her toward him. She closed her eyes—and waited for his kiss. She felt his breath, soft against her cheek, then he stepped back, still holding her hands in his.

"What is it, Marc? Tell me what you're thinking," she whispered.

"I don't know how, my lady."

He led her down a narrow footpath to a huge boulder. Lifting her up on it, he stood at her knees, his face turned up to hers.

"Yours are the bluest eyes I've ever seen. You asked me what I was thinking. I'll try to explain." His eyes held her attention. "I was remembering the many times I tried to change my ways. Every time I made a determined effort, I failed. Then—I met Someone—He changed me on the inside.

Carla gave a little jump and slid down the rock into his arms. Deliberately, she clung to him, then finally she pushed herself away. The silent hills echoed back the harshness of her laugh.

Back in the car, they continued up the steep mountainside, both stone-silent. Finally, Marc's words came, firm yet gentle. "I know I offended you. It wasn't my intention. I want you to hear me out. My experience may help you."

She wanted to stop him, but was compelled to listen.

"All my life I did as I pleased, more or less. I was handicapped a little with a widowed mother from the time I was about twenty-two. My father was killed in a plane crash."

Marc went on, almost doggedly. "I never married. I've been around. I'm not proud of that. Last year my life was completely changed, inwardly. I didn't do it. Someone greater than I did it. Do you know Who it was, Carla?"

"I suppose you're going to tell me it was Jesus Christ," she sneered. "My daughter talks about Him, begs me to let Him come into my heart." She shook her head, "But you—I can't believe this—a mature, intelligent man, what happened?"

He seemed calm, but Carla was aware of a new fire in his eyes. "I'd heard of Jesus all my life. My mother was a Christian. She and my aunt were brought up in a Christian home. Last year my mother insisted I take her to an evangelistic meeting in Pasadena. I didn't want to, but I thought—what harm could it do?"

Carla squirmed in her seat, turned her face to the window, and tried to close her ears.

"I went with her—are you listening?"

"I'm listening," she mumbled.

"That night at the meeting, I learned who I was and what I needed. I heard who Jesus Christ is, and what He had done for me. I invited Him into my life."

After that—silence. What did he expect her to say? How could a man, apparently in control of all his senses, talk like that? Well, she wasn't going to think about it now.

Hoping to end that kind of talk, she said, "Is your case here in Central City?"

They had just stopped in front of the Teller House.

"Not too far from here." Marc hopped out of the car. "I thought we'd stop and sightsee a while. Central City is booming this time of year."

"I've seen it many times." Carla pretended boredom. "Of course, I wasn't sightseeing. The gang likes to come up here after a dance in Idaho Springs for another round of drinks before we head back to Englewood."

She was sorry the minute the words were out of her mouth. Oh, well, that would put an end to a boring topic. She hooked her arm through his.

"Would you be my tour guide? Please, Mr. Randall?"

"I'd like nothing better, my lady. We might as well start here at the Teller House." He assumed the attitude of a lecturer.

"Back in 1873, President Ulysses S. Grant visited Central City." Carla watched passers-by stop and listen. Marc didn't seem embarrassed, so why should she be?

"When the city fathers knew he was coming," his voice boomed, "they wanted to do something spectacular. Gold was so common in those days, they sent to the mining town of Caribou

41

for silver bricks. They made a sidewalk from the curb to the entrance of Teller House of those silver bricks, just for the president to walk on."

Carla was impressed. She ran ahead of him up the steps. Stopping in front of him, she asked, "How do you know so much about this part of the country? You said you came from California."

"I lived around here when I was a young man. My mother and I stayed with my aunt right after my father died. I've been back several times since." He took her arm.

"Come on, Little Peanut, let's go inside now." She smiled at her new name.

"Now, this is the main reason I brought you here." They stopped before the swinging door. "I know you've seen it before—everybody has—but, do you know the history of it?"

They stepped inside. "Of course I've seen it," Carla said, "but I'd like to hear its history—especially from one so well-informed."

"The Face on the Barroom Floor was painted by an artist-newspaper man from Denver back in 1936. They say he and his lovely companion, Challis Walker, a sculptress, were attending a summer performance at the opera house. While they were here he painted her face on the barroom floor, and while he painted he recited the famous poem."

Carla felt squeamish. The room was small and musty. A spotlight shone on the picture on the floor, dim and faded after so many years. Neither Carla nor Marc spoke. She began to see herself in the image of the girl.

She tugged at Marc's arm. "Can we go now? I feel a little dizzy. Must be the altitude."

Back in the car Marc asked, "You okay?" She leaned back and nodded.

"You remind me of her," he smiled. "Same perpetual beauty—the kind of woman men fight over and even kill for." The compliment didn't please her.

They picked up speed on the steep upgrade. Except for winding curves just ahead, the view was cut off by dense underbrush on one side of the narrow road and sheer rock on the other.

"You didn't tell me where we're going."

"Have you heard of Winthrop House?"

"Matilda Winthrop's house? Of course, but I've never seen it. Is that where we're going?" Carla was excited.

She'd always admired Matilda Winthrop and was interested in what the society columns had to say about her. She often envied her many adventures. Suddenly her heart seemed to stop beating. Not more than a month ago she had read that Matilda Winthrop had died.

"Is that the case you're working on, Marc?"

He didn't answer. An eerie wave of foreboding swept over her, only to be dispelled the next instant by a breathtaking view just ahead of them. A long stretch of straight road gave a clear vision of the Winthrop House.

Bathed in the noonday sun, tall evergreens formed a backdrop for the picturebook house with its many gables. The white brick structure, capped by red-tiled roofing, gleamed with the promise of enchantment and mystery.

Wide expanses of lawn carpeted miles of leveled ground, like a country club golf course. Well-kept flower beds bordered the circular driveway. The beauty of the rose garden at the left of the wide steps took Carla's breath away.

Then, with quiet subtlety, a shadow seemed to creep over the scene. An uncanny silence chilled her flesh.

5

Marc's strange behavior increased her fears. He circled the driveway at five miles an hour, peering behind every shrub and corner. Finally, without a word he stopped, pulled her out of the car and swept her up the wide, shallow steps.

Unlocking the heavy carved door, he glanced over his shoulder, then pushed her into the entrance hall.

Once inside, all anxieties vanished. The solid stability of Winthrop House had been preserved through the years, along with the aristocracy of the Old West.

Carla's eyes swept over the exquisite parquet flooring of the huge entrance hall, its gleaming hardwood colors enhanced by the sunlight through the stained glass windows on either side of the door. Not a word had been spoken since that slow search along the circular driveway.

Marc tucked her hand under his arm and strolled the length of an immense Oriental-carpeted room. She was conscious of his noble bearing, even in casual sportswear. He seemed to belong to this crystal chandelier setting with its gold-flocked walls and gold-framed portraits.

At the grand staircase about halfway down the room, the decor changed from formal Victorian furnishings to contemporary comfort, accented by pieces of rare antiques.

Marc lit the logs in a marble and onyx fireplace. Carla watched the flames curl around the logs as they crackled their pungent pine fragrance. She was drawn to Marc's side. The glowing logs seemed to welcome her into his world.

Carla looked down at her feet and began to laugh. "Look— Lillian Russell would have been at home here—but, sneakers—"

Marc turned her toward him and tapped her nose with his forefinger. "I told you I like my women casual."

He stepped to the right of the fireplace and pulled a long, braided cord with a heavy silk tassel attached.

"Don't tell me—an English butler will magically appear."

"Wait and see." Her eyes followed his mysterious gaze where, at the far end of the room a small door opened and someone fluttered in.

"You rang, Mr. Randall?" Her eyes darted from Marc to Carla. Her nose flicked disapproval.

"This is Sarah Kerney. She and her husband, Walt, are caretakers here. Sarah, this is my friend, Mrs. Preston. We'd like a light lunch—anything you have will do."

Without comment, she disappeared behind the small door. Marc motioned Carla to the long, low couch.

With his back to the fireplace, he looked down at her. She squirmed under his gaze. Should she tuck her sneakers under her, or cross them sedately at the ankles?

To get his attention off her, she said, "Marc, why is everything so mysterious around here?"

He leaned over her, his face close to hers.

"What do you mean, Little Peanut?"

"You know what I mean. Why did you creep around the driveway before we came in? What were you looking for? And why is Sarah so unfriendly? And—why do you seem to belong here? The case you're on—it's Matilda Winthrop, isn't it? Marc—was she a relative?"

"My little detective." His eyes twinkled approval. "Yes, she was my aunt."

Suddenly without warning, he dashed across the room. She saw him throw open the door. He called, "Walt!" then closed the door behind him.

Everything was too quiet. The only sound she heard was crackling logs in the fireplace. Their warmth failed to stop the icy chill across her shoulders. She drew her feet up under her, and pressed further into the soft cushions. A sinister eeriness hovered over Winthrop House.

In an effort to bring her mind out of its numbed fear, she went to the mantel and admired the priceless curios. Genuine antiques. She didn't have one piece in her shop to compare with these.

From the corner of her eye she saw the tasseled cord, stepped over and impulsively pulled it. The small door opened almost immediately.

"You rang?" Sarah spoke sharply.

Carla swallowed. "Yes, I did. I'm concerned about Mr. Randall. Can you tell me where he is?"

"He's busy." She turned to leave.

"Just a minute." Carla cried out. "Tell him I must get back to Idaho Springs."

She grabbed her bag, slung it over her shoulder and perched on the edge of the couch, back stiff and ankles crossed. She stared at Sarah.

"Mr. Randall don't take orders from nobody!"

"Deliver my message!" Carla ordered.

Just then the front door flew open and Marc sprinted to her side.

"I didn't mean to be gone so long, Little Peanut. I'll take you home now." He lifted her to her feet.

Inside the long convertible, close beside him, conscious of his protective strength, she relaxed.

"Would you mind telling me why you left me alone in that spooky house?"

He reached for her hand and held it fondly. She saw the corner of his mouth quiver.

"What's so funny?" She jerked her hand away.

"You are. I've heard fire goes with red hair."

"My hair is not red. It's auburn." She began to laugh. "So, I do have a temper. Do you have an answer to my question?"

He reached for her hand again, and laid it between them on the seat.

"Remember I told you this morning I'd be mixing business with pleasure? Well, that was in the business category. It's in the 'secret file' for the present."

Icy fingers skimmed her shoulders again.

"So, you think Winthrop House is spooky, do you? Wait 'til you see the skeletons in our closets." He laughed.

By the time they got back to Irene's, it was almost two.

"I'll pick you up at eight. We'll watch the fireworks from Lookout Point."

She smiled as he ran down the steps. How nice that everything was cut and dried for her—no decisions to make.

Irene's voice startled her. "Jim's been calling all day. He sounds mad. He wants you to call him in his room."

"I guess he has reason to be a little excited." Carla dialed the number and waited for the connection to go through.

Jim's first words, "Where've you been?" put Carla on the defensive.

"Out, darling," she said cooly.

"What kind of an answer is that? I asked a simple question, but I didn't expect such a simple answer. Now I don't want to sound demanding, honey—but you promised we'd see a lot of each other up here."

"I know, darling." Carla was sad for a moment. There had never been angry words between them before. "It wasn't entirely my fault. I'll explain better when I see you."

"When's that?"

"I'll tell you what—meet me at the tavern across the street."

"Why don't you come to my room?"

"Oh, Jim, have you forgotten what I went through yesterday?" Her voice rose. "I won't be caught in a situation like that again."

"Okay, okay, have it your way. How long will it take you to get there?"

"A few minutes. See you."

Irene frowned at her. "You aren't going out again, are you? When do I get a few minutes of your precious time?"

Carla put her arms around Irene. "I'm so thoughtless. Please forgive me. My head is in a whirl. All this about Jim getting on his high horse, and that terrible scene with Mr. Barker last night. Let's talk while I change."

Irene's face brightened. "I'll fix us a drink." Carla stood in the doorway of the kitchen. "I can't think of anything but Marc. He's absolutely the most exciting man I've ever met!"

In the back bedroom, Carla sat on the bed and lifted her glass high.

"You won't believe this, Irene. I haven't had a drink all day. And come to think of it, I haven't even had a cigarette. What's happened to me?"

"Don't look so wild. You'll get over it."

"Do you think Marc has cast some sort of spell over me? I can't let that happen. Give me a cigarette."

She lit it. It tasted strange and made her dizzy. She put it out and set her drink on the dresser.

"Marc talks just like Penny—about Jesus, you know. It's very strange. He's so sensible about everything else."

"Maybe you should pay attention to him." Irene gulped her drink and reached for Carla's. "Then you could tell me what it's all about. It couldn't hurt either of us."

Carla dismissed the idea completely. "I have to meet Jim," she said.

"What are you gonna do about him? You mean an awful lot to him, you know. Isn't he planning to marry you when his wife divorces him?"

"Are you preaching, too? Don't waste any time on me. You've got a problem of your own."

Irene waved her hand. "Skip it, I think both of us have made a mess of our lives. But I don't know what we can do about it now." She turned at the door.

"You didn't tell me about Mr. Barker. George was upset when he came to bed—said Barker was threatening you."

"I'll tell you about it later. I've got to run now."

In the dingy, dark tavern across the street, it took a few minutes to focus her eyes on Jim, slumped at the bar. After she tapped his shoulder, he got up and staggered to a booth. He grabbed her hands and held them as if he were afraid she might get away.

"It's been too long, honey," he whined.

"I know, darling. I'm truly sorry about last night."

"What happened to you, anyway? Where did you go? And who was that guy with you?"

"Darling, trust me. Would you like me to drive you home this afternoon? We could talk while you sober up."

"I'm not drunk. Besides, I don't have to be back 'til tomorrow. Sue already knows."

Why did she feel a twinge of jealousy? "You called her?" she asked.

"If you'd been with me, I would never have thought of it."

"That's all right, Jim. Maybe someday we'll know what we want—both of us."

Carla slid out of the booth. Jim staggered to his feet and took her in his arms.

"You know I want you, honey, and nobody else."

"We can wait," she whispered. "Call me in the morning before you leave."

Out in the sunlight, a wave of pity swept over her as she left him standing alone, so hopelessly young.

Before she crossed the street, she saw Mr. Barker's car parked in front of her sister's house. She'd have to face him, too. Squaring her shoulders, she marched up the steps.

George opened the door for her. "Hi, Sis, I was just going to get you." He grinned and left her alone with Mr. Barker.

Carla leaned against the front door and hoped the fear in her heart wouldn't show in her face. He sat in a big chair, the man who had seemed mentally unbalanced the night before, now apparently in full control of all emotion. Through draped eyes and loose lips, he said. "Well, Carla, my dear, it's been interesting, to say the least. Of course, we'll continue along on a friendly basis."

He struggled to his feet and offered a small, soft hand. She forced herself to take it.

"Thank you for bringing me up here," she said. "As for continuing on a friendly basis, we'll see about that later. At any rate, I won't be back in Englewood for at least a week." She stepped to one side to let him pass through the door.

"You'll be hearing from me, my dear," he rasped.

Carla felt dirty. She ran down the hall to her room, threw herself on the bed and kicked off her shoes. Irene came in.

"What was that all about? I couldn't hear everything."

"Well, they're both in their places for the time being." She sat up and laughed. "There's nothing like an uncluttered life. One man at a time, I always say." She jumped up, slipped out of her dress and headed for the shower.

"Be out in a jiffy," she called.

In the privacy of the shower, Carla dismissed all other events and allowed Marc's image to invade every corner of her mind. The rest of the day she waited for eight o'clock.

At last, on Lookout Point she was at his side. From the rock wall, a million stars twinkled above the lights of the small mountain town.

"The heavens declare the glory of God." Marc's voice was filled with wonder. "And the firmament sheweth his handiwork." Folded in his arms, she heard their hearts pound in unison.

"My sweet Little Peanut," he whispered in her hair. Then, deliberately, he tucked her hand under his arm and strolled back to the car. He helped her in and stood by the open door, apparently in full control of his feelings.

"We'll watch from here. We'll see how man's puny efforts will strive in competition with the beauty of God's universe."

Carla wasn't interested in competitions. All she wanted was to hear Marc say he loved her, and to feel his lips on hers. Why did there have to be a wall between them?

He got in on the driver's side and pulled her close to him, his arm over her shoulder.

"I've got to go back to Winthrop House tomorrow. I'd like to have you with me." Carla stiffened. "Before you decide, let me tell you why I have to go back. I told you I'm an insurance investigator. Aunt Matilda had her policy with our company. The president of the company isn't satisfied with the coroner's report." Carla shuddered.

His arm tightened on her shoulder. "Everything has to be cleared up before the estate can be settled. There can be no doubts."

"Are there real doubts?" she whispered.

"I've uncovered a few things. Detective work can be a little sticky. I'll understand if you don't want to go."

"But I do." She clung to his arm.

"How would you like to be my assistant?" She knew his eyes twinkled.

"I'll be anything you want me to be," she said seriously.

"Very well, my Dear Watson, it's all set. Now, before I list my findings up to this point, I feel I should let you know the truth."

Without a hint of flippancy, he spoke in a low monotone. "I have sufficient reason to believe my aunt did not die of natural causes."

6

Carla Preston stuck her head in the kitchen door. "Coffee smells good," she said.

"You're up early. Want an eye-opener?" Irene poured whiskey in a cup.

"Not this early. I will take a cup of coffee, straight."

She studied her sister's face. "Irene, what's wrong?"

"Is this polite conversation, or are you really interested?"

"Now, what kind of a question is that? You know I've always been interested in you."

"I thought you were, but do you realize I haven't had so much as an hour alone with you?"

"Well, I'm here now, so tell me what's the matter."

"This town. George. Everything."

"Why don't you come home with me for awhile?"

Irene's eyes widened. "Do you mean it? I'd love to. But, what about Mother? I think she's coming home today."

"Can't she stay here and cook for George? Just tell her I need a ride home."

"I almost forgot. Penny called here last night. Said it's important for you to call her. Something about your house."

Carla called the home of the friend where Penny was staying, and after a short wait Carla asked, "Penny, are you all right?"

"I'm okay. The real estate man wants you to get in touch with him—something about the deal for the house falling through."

How could that be? It was in escrow! Carla was stunned.

"Mom—did you hear? Are you okay?"

"It's all right, Penny. I'll take care of it."

"He said Mr. Barker cancelled out. Was he the buyer, Mom?"

Carla's throat tightened. She didn't know that. Was this the way he was going to get even?

"I'm coming home next Wednesday, Penny. Bye."

In a monotone she told Irene what had happened.

"You don't have to sell, do you, Sis?"

"Not really, but that's not the point. Do you realize the influence that man has? It scares me."

"What are you gonna do?"

"I don't know. I have to get away from Englewood."

Irene's laugh was bitter. "That's funny. We both want to leave town. I wonder if it'd change anything?"

"But I've got to do something," Carla wailed. "I'm just a crowd-follower—in a rut—especially with Jim. What do you think I should do?"

"Why don't you marry Marc?"

Carla closed her eyes and shook her head. "He hasn't even kissed me. And I don't think he will. Don't ask me why."

"Maybe it's because he's religious," said Irene.

"Could be. There's a wall between us—just like with Penny. Maybe I do need what they have."

"I think Mother has it. I haven't had a chance to tell you. Ever since she started going to that little church across the street from the hotel—you've seen it . . ."

"Oh, yes," said Carla. "I've always liked the way it looks. So little—and a bell tower, with a cross on top. When did Mother start going there?"

"It was the Sunday after your birthday. I remember 'cause when she got home from church that day, she said she wished she hadn't given you that book for your birthday. Said she was going to tell you not to read it. It wasn't the right way to think."

"When is she coming home?"

"Today, I think. Are you gonna be here?"

"Not 'til later. I'm going to Winthrop House again."

Carla slipped into faded blue jeans, a striped top, and stepped into her sneakers. A royal-blue scarf held her curls high on top of her head.

"No wonder Marc won't kiss you," grinned Irene. "He probably thinks he'd be contributing to juvenile delinquency."

"He likes his women causal," Carla smiled. "You don't know how silly I feel dressed like this in that mansion."

"What's it like? I've always wanted to see it."

"Simply elegant. It's hard to describe, but there's something eerie about it, too. I really don't want to go back, but I have to be with Marc."

At the sound of the doorbell, she called over her shoulder, "Tell Mother I'll see her this evening."

Marc waited at the foot of the steps. Shallow-breathed, she gave him her hand. Would she ever be able to look at him matter-of-factly, without her heart jumping into her throat?

Behind the wheel of his car, he pulled her close to his side. "Looks like we're in for a storm, Little Peanut."

She clung to his arm. "I'm scared. I wonder what today will bring?"

"This is the day the Lord has made—there's no earthly reason to be afraid."

She ignored his rhyme-making. "You won't leave me alone again, will you?"

"I won't," he promised.

The drive to Central City looked bright, even through black, threatening clouds.

"What do you expect to find today?" Carla asked.

"Who knows? The Shadow knows," he teased. "Seriously, I'd be satisfied just to get a few questions answered."

At the end of the narrow, winding road, Carla gazed at the majestic, picture book house. It seemed to stand in bas-relief against a backdrop of low-hanging clouds and dense evergreens.

"Marc, why does Winthrop House have so many gables?"

"That many rooms were added to the original structure," he explained. "At one time it was a modest seven-room house. When the girls—my mother and Aunt Matilda—got in their teens, my grandfather began adding more rooms. I think he expected them to marry and fill Winthrop House with grandchildren! My grandfather was a very romantic character." He glanced down at her upturned face.

Carla pressed closer to him. "Would you say some of his blood runs in your veins, Marc Randall?"

"What would you say?" he asked.

What was she supposed to say? She changed the subject. "Matilda must have inherited your grandfather's spirit of adventure. I've read of her many romances abroad and on the west coast. Did she ever marry?"

"No. She was engaged to be married when she was just seventeen. Her fiance was killed the day before their wedding. She saw it happen. He was thrown from a horse just outside her window."

Carla shivered. "What a tragedy."

Suddenly, she noticed Marc was circling the driveway at five miles an hour again, his eyes darting behind every shrub.

"What are you looking for?" Carla clenched his arm.

"One never knows, does one?"

Before she could retort, a jagged streak of lightning slashed the sky, followed by a clap of thunder. She threw her arms around Marc's neck and screamed.

He jumped out of the car, dragging her with him, bounded up the steps, and crossed the wide veranda. At the front door, another crash of thunder rumbled the floor beneath them.

Inside, the heavy carved door muffled the storm. Clinging to his arm, Carla ran to keep up with his long strides. At the marble fireplace, she knelt close to him as he lit the logs. Then gently he pulled her down beside him on the white fur rug. For a while they watched the flames leap and curl up the chimney, then he jumped up and gave a quick jerk of the tasseled cord.

"How about some tea and crumpets?" She didn't answer. She wanted to say something sarcastic, like "why not, that's a fine pastime." Instead, she pretended interest in her first experience with a crumpet.

She jumped to her feet as Sarah's voice chirped from the far corner of the room. She felt Sarah's eyes stab through the shadows, and she shivered in spite of herself.

Next to her on the couch, Marc stretched his legs as his arm rested behind her head. "This is what I call living," he sighed, "—sheltered from the raging storm, sitting by a cozy fire with a beautiful little peanut nestled close beside me."

"I'm glad you feel at home here. It isn't what I'd call cozy." Carla hugged herself.

"You'll get used to it."

What did he mean? Should she allow her heart to race like that?

Sarah's birdlike movements interrupted Carla's hopes. Fascinated, she watched Sarah's small head flick from side to side while keeping a constant eye on Carla. When the door closed behind Sarah, Carla was able to breathe again.

"What's the matter, Little Peanut? You seem nervous."

"Just watching her gives me the jitters." She poured their tea and tasted a crumpet.

"Do you like it? You can't beat Sarah's cooking."

"It's good—tastes like toasted pancakes."

Marc put his cup down. "We'll visit the Kerneys later. I'm sure Sarah will be friendlier in her own domain."

When he pulled her to her feet, her fingers tingled as he held her hands against his chest. She closed her eyes and held her breath, her lips close to his.

"Little Peanut," he whispered against her cheek, "don't think I'm leading you on. When the time is right, I'll let you know my plans."

With his finger, he slowly outlined her profile, starting at her forehead, across her nose and lips, under her chin, and down to the hollow of her throat. Then, thrusting his hands in his hip pockets, he strolled back to the fireplace and turned his face toward the dying embers.

Humiliated and frustrated, Carla raced across the expanse of Oriental carpeting. A strange darkness and gloom suffocated her. Reaching the front wall, she searched for windows. A light tug on a beaded cord parted heavy, velvet drapes.

Motionless before the huge plate glass window, Carla watched silver strips of light slash the stormy sky, only to be swallowed up by everchanging, black clouds.

The scene depicted her own stormy past, pierced by flashes of hope, only to be overshadowed by clouds of doubt and disappointment again.

She felt his presence before his arms encircled her. "Don't be unhappy, Little Peanut," he whispered. Her back stiffened.

"Let's visit the Kerneys now." He tucked her hand under his arm. "Remember, you're still my super-sleuth. On the alert, Dr. Watson. There's work to be done."

Guiding her toward the small door in the far corner of the room, their comradery was partially restored. He put a little black notebook and pen in her hand.

"Watch for clues, my good man. Jot down anything that might seem out of place or out of the ordinary."

"The largest kitchen Carla had ever seen was on the other side of the small door. Copper-bottomed pans shone from one wall. Directly below the pans were the most modern utilities: microwave oven, electric grill, slow cooker, toaster, waffle iron, electric frying pan—all conveniently placed on a long counter.

The opposite wall was occupied with built-ins: sink, garbage disposal, dishwasher, trash compactor, and refrigerator-freezer. The spotless display amazed Carla.

Waving toward the copper-bottomed pans, Marc said, "As you can see, Sarah takes her job seriously. I don't know how she does it. The whole house is kept up the same way."

"How long did you say the Kerneys have been here?"

"About ten years, I think. Aunt Matilda liked them very much. Said they minded their own business and left hers alone."

At that moment, Carla saw something that was certainly out of place in Sarah's immaculate kitchen. She ran across the room and picked up a scrap of paper from the floor beside the trash compactor.

"What is it, Watson?" Marc looked over her shoulder. "It looks like Aunt Matilda's writing."

"What does it mean—'R. Pow.' and 'pd.'?" asked Carla. Marc took the slip of paper and turned it over.

"It must be sums of money. Too bad the first numbers have been torn off. You can see they were large amounts by the three zeros before the decimal point."

"By Jove, Holmes, would you say it's our first clue?"

"Indubitably, Dr. Watson."

"The next question that crosses my mind," said Carla, "is not How did it get here? but rather, How did it stay here in Sarah's immaculate kitchen?"

Marc beamed on her. "I knew you'd make a good detective. Good work. Keep alert. There are yet more clues to be uncovered."

Sarah met Marc and Carla at the door of her apartment with a dust cloth in her hand.

"It's a pleasure Mr. Randall. Do come in and make yourselves at home." She flitted about the room, shifting neatly stacked magazines from one place to another.

"I just put the kettle on. You'll stay for tea, won't you?" She flicked imaginary dust from a table top.

"I thought I heard your voice, Mr. Randall." Walt came through the back door, bowed and removed an old felt hat from his grizzled head. "How be ya?" he asked.

"Fine thanks, Walt. This is Mrs. Preston."

"Mornin', Ma'am. Glad to know ya."

Sarah brought in a tray of cups and a teapot. She set a plate of crumpets next to Marc. Carla was aware of her devoted attention to him.

"The crumpets we had earlier were delicious," said Carla.

Sarah ignored her. Marc looked puzzled. He leaned over and covered both Sarah's and Walt's hands with his.

"Folks," he said, "you know why I'm here. It's about Aunt Matilda. I don't want you to be afraid to tell me anything you can think of that might help." He nodded toward Carla. "Mrs. Preston is on the case with me."

"Sarah's eyebrows disappeared under her short, straight bangs. Marc glanced at Carla and smiled reassuringly, then continued, "We don't know for sure yet, but all the evidence so far points to the fact that she didn't die of natural causes."

Carla saw Walt's face blanch. He set his cup down. "I told ya Sarah—I told ya there'd be questions." He rocked back and forth, mumbling something under his breath.

Sarah jumped up and fluttered over him. "Walt, you quit that. There ain't nothin' we can tell."

7

Marc Randall's eyes flashed at Sarah.

"Let me warn you both; it's illegal to withhold evidence."

Walt peered from under bushy brows. "I didn't like the guy from the first," he muttered.

"Walt's suspicious of any good-lookin' feller," Sarah interrupted. "An this'n was more'n good-lookin'. Tall an' straight, he was. An' sech manners! Miss 'Tilda took to him like a honeybee."

"That's jest it," said Walt. "How could a good-lookin' guy like that make over a little ol' woman like Miss 'Tilda? Beggin' pardon, Mr. Randall."

"You're right, Walt," Marc smiled. "Unless he had an ulterior motive." He unfolded the scrap of paper Carla had found on the kitchen floor. "Does this mean anything to you?"

Sarah frowned and set her lips in a pink line. Walt opened his mouth, then closed it.

"Remember what I said about withholding evidence."

"She found it." Walt pointed his thumb at Sarah. "They was some papers in the wastepaper basket in the master bedroom. When she went to put 'em in the trash, she seen writin' on 'em."

"Hush up, Walt."

"She brought 'em in here an' we both looked at 'em. But she was the nosy one."

"They was all Greek to us." Sarah flipped her head. "So I put 'em all in the trash. This'n musta fell out."

Marc turned the paper over. "What does this mean, R. Pow.?"

"That's him," blurted Sarah. "Ronald Powell's his name. I seen it on a letter that come here for him. Had a Denver postmark on it. Warn't no return address."

"Did Ronald Powell ever stay here overnight?"

"Several nights." The drooped corners of her mouth showed her disapproval. "Slept in the master bedroom."

"Thanks, folks, you've helped a lot."

As they left Carla clung to Marc's hand.

"Oh, Marc, I'm scared. It's so mysterious. Who do you think Ronald Powell is? Where did he come from? Where is he now?"

"Calm down, Little Peanut. Right now we'll take a look at the master bedroom." Carla held back. "Come now, I can't get along without my assistant. Be alert, Dr. Watson."

"Very well, Holmes."

At the foot of the wide stairway, fear clutched her throat as she let her eyes follow the steps to the top. Was this the same flight of stairs she'd seen in her nightmare? She dismissed the thought.

At the top, Carla looked over the banister. "What a view from here! You can see the fireplace and the entire living room to those sliding doors. What's in that room, Marc?"

"It's used for very special occasions. You'll see it later. Right now it's business before pleasure."

She had to quicken her pace to keep up with his walk down the hall to the master bedroom. Marc stopped suddenly. Was it because the door stood open? He took a quick look inside and motioned her in.

"We'll proceed with the investigation," he said.

Carla's gaze lingered on the furnishings of the immense room: king-sized bed, highboy, massive rolltop desk. All were made from elaborately carved oak.

"Quite a display of male chauvinism," she said.

Marc chuckled as he began his search through every drawer in the room. He opened the wardrobe doors and stepped inside. From where she stood, nothing was visible but a few empty hangers.

Coming out of the wardrobe he said, "Well, if there were any clues, Sarah has thoroughly removed them."

He closed the door, locked it, and stepped briskly down the hall, Carla's hand in his. At the first door beyond the landing, he stopped.

"As long as we're here, you might as well see this room."

She watched him unlock the door, and swinging it wide, he bowed over her hand. "Enter, my lady, into the private realm of the late Matilda Winthrop."

Blood drained from her heart. A film came over her eyes. She stumbled toward the balcony. Horror and nausea enveloped her.

She clung to the railing above the stairway.

Marc touched her arm, then cupped her face in his hands. She felt his warm breath on her cheek.

"My Little Peanut, I'm so sorry," he whispered in her ear. He nestled her head under his chin and folded her close to his chest. She felt his heart beat in rhythm with her own. Suspended in timeless silence, they were transfixed in a statue-embrace. She was aware of new strength and courage that seemed to flow from him.

Carla opened her eyes and smiled. "May I see her room now?"

His eyes opened wide, then that crinkled smile appeared. "As you wish, my lady."

Slowly, they moved back down the thick-carpeted hallway to the open door that led into the late Matilda Winthrop's private domain.

This time Carla steeled herself against her fear of death, and tried to objectively observe the beauty of this ultra-feminine room. She unconsciously compared it to the masculinity of the master bedroom they had just left.

Carla approved of Matilda's taste in decorating. The room was furnished with gold and antique white French Provincial furniture. The carpeting was thick-piled white plush.

Her eyes were drawn to the wall behind the head of the bed. A giant handpainted mural depicted a flower garden. Soft lavender tones gave the illusion of mist falling upon the garden. In the foreground, myriads of violets, each petal delicately precise, ranged in color tones from pale pink to deep purple. Her eyes swept on down to the lavender satin bedspread, intricately embroidered. The violets seemed to sprinkle the bed with their perfume.

Marc's soft voice brought Carla out of her self-inflicted trance. "Come over here, Peanut. I want you to see this."

Noiselessly, a huge mirrored door slid open. The inside revealed row upon row of elegant gowns of every description and color.

"My aunt loved to dress up. I guess you'd call her extravagant."

Carla was awed as she touched the fine fabrics—satin, crisp taffeta, lace and chiffon. Her fingers tingled with the sense of vibrancy created by the sparkling trimmings of rhinestones, feathers and gold braid.

"She must have looked lovely, Marc. I wish I could have met her in person, but just being among her possessions gives me a sense of warmth and love for her."

Marc lifted one of the gowns from its hanger, and stepping behind Carla, held it up to her shoulders.

"I thought you were about the same size." His eyes twinkled approval.

"It's the most beautiful dress I've ever seen!" Almost reverently she fitted it to her waist, and watched the white, brocaded-satin folds touch the floor.

"I pictured her taller," she said.

"No, she was a little peanut, too. She never got to wear it."

"This was her wedding dress?"

He nodded and slowly put the dress back on the hanger.

After he closed the wardrobe door, he led Carla to the window, held back the filmy drapes and said, "See that bare space in the hedgerow? She had it cut down after her fiance was killed. He was thrown from his horse while trying to clear it." Carla shivered.

Marc let the drapes fall into place and pointed to a gold-framed, oval portrait on the wall next to the window.

"I'm sure she had many admirers, even when this portrait was made on her last birthday. She was seventy last January. I guess she never got over her first love."

"She was beautiful even at seventy," said Carla. After a long pause, she said, "Marc, where did she die?"

"That's one of the reasons for our investigation. The coroner's report states she died in her bed from possible natural causes."

Carla could see the small, dead body of Matilda Winthrop lying on the lavender satin bedspread. Blindly she fled from the room, across the hall and down the stairway.

Somehow Marc reached the bottom step before she did and caught her in his arms. She broke away from him, ran to the couch, swung her bag over her shoulder and rushed for the front door.

In the car she struggled for composure. Why was she such a

coward? What was Marc thinking? Why didn't he say something?

Minutes passed before he swung into the wide space in the road where they had stopped before. Stepping out of the car, he reached for her hand. They slipped over the same pine needles, and at the same huge boulder, he lifted her on it, and stood at her knees once again.

Sunlight filtered through tall pine trees, casting shadows across his handsome face. His clear eyes searched hers.

"Tell me, Carla, are you afraid of death?"

"Desperately," she choked.

"Are you afraid to die?"

"Isn't everyone?"

"Do you believe there's life after death?"

"I hope not." She brushed a strand of hair from her forehead. "I suppose you believe in Heaven and Hell."

"I do, Carla."

"Oh, Marc! I believe you make your own Heaven or Hell right here on earth. I can't believe anything else."

She slid down the rock into his arms.

"You're a stubborn woman." He smiled, but Carla saw a hint of sadness in his eyes.

Why did it mean so much to him that she believe as he did? She didn't care if he wanted to believe such strange things, but why force these ideas on her? It was downright maddening!

"Maybe we should stop seeing each other," she spoke flippantly.

"If that's what you want." Marc looked serious.

She threw her arms around his neck. "Oh, no, Marc. I have to be with you."

They both laughed nervously and clung to each other on the way back to the car.

Carla's heart sank again when she realized they were heading back to Winthrop House.

"Just remembered something important," he said. "Sarah can fix our lunch. I promise we'll go somewhere extra special for dinner tonight. Is that satisfactory with you, Dr. Watson?"

Determined to hide her fears, Carla said, "Anywhere with you is all right with me, Mr. Holmes."

She closed her eyes and tried to think of something nice about Winthrop House—rows of exquisite gowns behind mirrored sliding doors captured her mind.

"Marc, do you think I could try on one of Aunt Matilda's dresses?"

"Do you mean that?" he asked. "You never cease to amaze me, Peanut. I thought you'd never go near the place again. And now you say you want to try on one of her dresses! What made you change your mind?"

"Must be my incurable romantic nature. I can imagine myself as Matilda Winthrop—fascinating, beautiful, desirable." Carla sighed.

"And it doesn't bother you that she's dead—that she might have died in that very room?"

Why did he say those things? Was it because he wanted her to accept reality?

She flashed a slightly shaky smile at him. "Thanks, Marc, I appreciate your concern. But we wouldn't want the word to get around that Watson was a coward, would we? Besides," she set her jaw, "might as well face it."

A little later in Matilda's room, Carla ran to the mirrored doors, slid them open, and took the wedding gown from its hanger.

She turned to Marc, "I'm sure it's just my size. Do you want me to try it on?"

"You know I do. I'll wait outside. Call when you're ready."

With shallow breaths, she stepped out of her clothes. As the heavy satin folds slipped over her head, the present seemed to fade as shadows of the past came into view. Matilda Winthrop came to life in her reflection. Carla spoke to her.

"Thank you, Aunt Matilda, for letting me try it on. I'm sorry you didn't get to wear it."

She was jolted back to the present. No zipper! How could she manage all those hooks and eyes? She'd never hooked an eye in her life. Opening the door she called to Marc. No answer. Outside in the hall she called. "Marc, where are you? I need you."

From the banister, a flicker of light from the fireplace was visible, but where was Marc? Clutching the back of the gown together with one hand, and holding the skirt up with the other, she raced down the long flight of stairs.

At the far end of the couch, bent over a letter he held under a lamp, Marc looked startled when she appeared beside him. The gown had slipped from one shoulder.

Then he began to laugh. "Looks like you ran into a little problem."

He put the letter down, turned her around and started hooking eyes. As he finished the task, he held her at arm's length and smiled his approval.

"It was made for you, my Little Peanut."

Carla took a few steps in front of him, turned, and wing-fashion, spread the skirt shoulder-high. In one long stride, Marc was beside her. He bent his elbow, placed her hand on top of his and slow-stepped across the room as he hummed the wedding march. Carla closed her eyes. In her imagination she was young Matilda Winthrop on her wedding day with her young lover who was Marc, of course.

He stopped at the foot of the staircase and bowed over her hand. "My lady, I'm impressed, enchanted, enslaved. How many valiant men have fallen under your charms?"

He drew her close, unhooked the top hooks on the gown, turned her toward the steps and said, "You can manage the rest. Hurry back."

Breathless with excitement, she lifted her skirt high, holding the back closed, and raced up the stairs. She flung herself on Matilda's satin-covered bed. Her heart shook her chest, her arms ached, breathing was labored. Why, this kind of excitement could bring on a heart attack!

She bolted upright. That was it! A heart attack! Matilda was old. If she had experienced this kind of exertion and emotional upheaval—of course it would be diagnosed as natural causes at her age.

Carla slipped out of the dress and as it came over her head she caught the inescapable scent of violets. She held the neckline to her nose—her throat tightened. Could a fragrance linger for fifty years?

Carla threw the dress on the bed, jumped into her clothes and from the balcony screamed, "Marc, Marc, I've found another clue."

Bounding up the stairs, he was soon behind her. She swept the gown up to his face. "Right there. Smell right there. Would you say it's perfume? Violet perfume?"

"I'd say you're right, Dr. Watson. What are your deductions?" He knew how to relieve a tense situation.

"I'm glad you asked, Holmes. The question uppermost in my mind is, Could even the most potent perfume leave its fragrance over a period of fifty years? The answer is quite obvious, Mr. Holmes. The gown has been worn recently, of course."

Marc grinned, "Precisely correct."

She hung the dress back in the wardrobe while Marc began to search dresser drawers.

"Here they are," he called. "I knew there'd be a place for her fine perfumes. Here's the glass-bottomed drawer. And here's the violet perfume."

Carla took the cut glass crystal bottle from his hand and gasped at its exquisite beauty. She lifted the elaborate stopper and waved it under her nose.

"It's the same—and look at the label on the bottom. 'Violette Parfum, Made in Paris'." Carla brushed her cheek with the bottle. "Aunt Matilda was partial to violets, wasn't she?"

"I never thought of it before. You're right, of course." His eyes followed hers to the mural behind the violet-sprinkled bedspread.

Carla put the bottle back in the drawer. "Why did she wear her wedding gown? Was it for the stranger, Ronald Powell? Was she in love with him? Could the emotional stimuli have been too much for her?"

Marc began to chuckle as he steered her across the room. He led her through the door and locked it.

"Enough, my dear Watson. Your deductions and questions are too much for me."

At the top of the stairs, Carla's eyes suddenly widened as they swept the area below. The sliding doors of the mystery room were open.

8

From the doorway of the mystery room, Carla Preston breathed in the faint mustiness of Old World aristocracy, her love for antiques satisfied.

"Is this that special occasion?" she asked.

She saw the corners of his mouth crinkle. "Not necessarily, but it's a good place to eat."

Carla gazed at the intimate room, its crystal chandelier sending prismatic colors across the white Irish linen cloth. The round dining table was properly set with exquisite silver and crystal.

Swallowed in a huge, high-backed chair, hands clasped in her lap, Carla's eyes continued their feast of lavish furnishings: rich Oriental rug, glowing walnut paneling, wine-colored velvet drapes. There was the "Old Masters" framed in antique gold, and massive shelves lined with leather-bound volumes.

Her gaze came back and settled on the man across the table. "Your presence complements the setting, Mr. Randall."

Could he read her heart? "I love you," she whispered.

Instantly he was behind her chair. Tilting her chin, he looked deep into her eyes, and in a low voice said, "You make me very happy."

That was all! Then, back at his place, he bowed his head and thanked "Our Heavenly Father" for all His blessings.

Thick silence stood between them. Humiliated, Carla's ears burned; her throat tightened. He could have said he loved her, too! She wished she'd never met him; yet, she knew she loved him. Sarah's entrance was a welcome interruption.

Marc rose and casually dropped his napkin at the side of his plate, "It was a fine lunch, Sarah. Thank you."

He pulled Carla's chair out, tucked her hand under his arm—a gesture becoming more and more familiar to her—and guided her to the fireplace.

Carla was unable to hide her frustration from Marc, and was glad when he resumed his detective role, aware of his attempt to ease tensions.

Elaborately, he spread a letter out on the coffee table in front of them. "Tell me, Dr. Watson, what do you make of this?"

Eyes blurred with unshed tears, she entered her role half-heartedly.

"Confidentially, Holmes, I can't make head or tail of it."

"Nor I, my dear Watson. Obviously, it was addressed to our mystery man, Ronald Powell. Observe the envelope."

Carla, more relaxed now, examined it thoroughly. "Have you detected the unusual features of the letter, Mr. Holmes?" Carla waved the letter under Marc's nose.

"You will note there is no salutation and no signature. We assume, of course, it was written to Ronald Powell, but who wrote it?"

"A gross oversight, to be sure," Marc beamed at her.

"Seriously, Marc, where did you get the letter? It's the same one you were looking at under the lamp, isn't it?"

"That's right; I didn't tell you. Sarah gave it to me. She took it from Ronald Powell's suitcase. Her excuse—she didn't trust the man and wanted to find out more about him."

"Why didn't she turn it over to the police?"

"Afraid, I guess." He showed the envelope to her again.

"Look at the postmark—Denver, Colorado, May 27, 2:00 P.M. Of course, that doesn't prove the writer lived in Denver. Now— examine the contents of the letter."

She read aloud, "I am not waiting much longer. If you are not here by Friday, that is it." After a slight pause, "What day was May twenty-seventh?"

He took a calendar card from his wallet. "May twenty-seventh was a Friday. Looks like our man Powell was given a deadline." *Deadline*—Carla shivered.

"What was the date of your aunt's death?"

"June third." His hand began to tremble as he checked the calendar. "That was the deadline date—Friday, June third."

Icy fingers slid over the back of her neck. "Oh, Marc, we're not playing games, are we?"

She took the little black notebook from her purse. "Let's compare our entries. My first is: Clue number one—Scrap of

67

paper found by trash compactor. 'R. Pow.' and 'pd.' on one side; on the other, a column of zeros, first digits torn off. My notation, 'evidently large sums of money'. Is that your first clue, Marc?"

"Almost word for word. My second entry is the letter, the postmark and contents. Do you have that?"

"Not yet. May I copy yours?" As she copied from his notebook, she was conscious of his movements as he placed another log on the fireplace.

She made her thoughts come back to the notebook. "I have one more entry. Do you want to hear it?"

He dropped on the couch beside her, his head resting on the back, legs stretched out in front. "I'm glad you're my assistant. Proceed."

"Clue number three: Violet fragrance detected on neckline of wedding dress. Crystal bottle labeled, 'Violette Parfum, Made in Paris' found in dresser drawer."

Marc jumped to his feet. "There's one more thing I have to take care of today. It shouldn't take too long. Walt and Sarah are in their apartment. Rest while I'm gone." He kissed her forehead and was gone before she could protest.

A weighty silence fell over the house, yet there seemed to be an eerie movement about it. Carla envisaged Matilda's girlhood. She pictured the large room crowded with people; beautiful ladies in elegant gowns and glittering jewels, handso,ne men in full-dress tuxedos with ruffled shirt fronts.

Coming out of her daydream, she was surprised to find herself at Matilda's bedroom door. A question, deep in the shadows of her mind, demanded an answer. Where were the Winthrop jewels? Every wealthy family possessed heirlooms and precious gems of some kind. Marc hadn't mentioned them. She'd surprise him by a little private investigation of her own.

She rolled back the mirrored doors, and marveled again at the array of splendor. She would never get her fill of feasting on the exquisite gowns dating back fifty years—bygone years of romance and galantry.

The jewels could be somewhere in the huge wardrobe. Carefully she pushed the gowns to one end of the long rod. Rows of shoe boxes were exposed. She got on her knees to read the labels—every color imaginable—and to her amazement saw Matilda's shoe size was five and a half.

The temptation was too great. Removing her sneakers, she selected white satin high-heels, adorned with enormous rhinestone buckles. A perfect fit. She jumped up and danced about the room, viewing herself in the mirrored doors. What a sight! Faded jeans, striped top—and Cinderella slippers.

Startled by her own laughter, she stepped out of the shoes and replaced them in the box. On her knees again, her eyes strained for the empty space to put the box. Her breath caught in her throat. There it was! An ornate chest of lustrous carved onyx, banded in pure gold, and closed with a jeweled clasp. Her hands trembled as she lifted it from its hiding place.

On the floor, the box in her lap, she lifted the lid. Stacked on top of each other were three velvet-lined drawers. Carla's fingers caressed the priceless strands of pearls that lay in the top drawer. She could almost feel the warm glow of their lustrous tones—rose, silver and creamy-white. They were all shapes—ovals, teardrops and circles.

At the point of lifting the top drawer, her eyes rested on something noticeably out of place among the oceans of pearls. A man's ring—richly-carved jade, set in brushed gold. Carla ran to the dressing table lamp for a closer examination. What an unusual design! A clearly sculptured ram's head covered the entire surface of the jade gemstone. Framing the ram's head were twisted strands of gold representing a hunter's bow. A silver arrow pierced through the ears of the ram. The tip of the arrow sparkled with a single, blood-red ruby. Carla closed her eyes. Where had she seen it before?

She slipped the ring on her thumb and flew back to the chest. Settled on the floor and again ready to lift the lid, a cold draft on the back of her neck blew over her shoulder. In that instant, the chest was snatched from her lap, accompanied by a hissing sound in her ear.

"What d'ya think you're doin' with Miss 'Tilda's things? We been lookin' for this." Sarah swished from the room.

"Just a minute," Carla stammered. She grabbed her sneakers from the floor where she'd left them while trying on Matilda's slippers. She reached the bottom of the stairs in time to see Sarah disappear behind the small door in the corner of the room.

Angry and indignant, she marched back to the couch. She'd tell Marc about this! She stared at the dead coals in the fireplace. Why didn't he come back?

Muffled rolls of thunder made her body shiver. She raced across the immense room and looked out the front window. His car was gone. He hadn't told her he was leaving the grounds!

She hugged herself, fighting against hysteria. A quick glance toward the intimate dining room revealed a large stereo just outside the sliding doors. She ran over to it, switched the On button and fled back to the fireplace.

Curled in the corner of the couch, she listened to a man's voice, low and resonant, drifting from the stereo. The words were clear, strange, but convincing. "Ask the Lord what you will and He will answer speedily." Anything? Could that really be true?

With hands clasped under her chin, she whispered, "Please, God, send Marc back."

Instantly, the front door flew open. Marc ran toward her. Carla stood and stared in amazement.

"It took longer than I thought. Are you all right?"

Carla buried her face in his chest. "God answered me. Listen."

"Ask the Lord what you will—and He will answer—speedily." The words of the song filled the room.

"Did you hear it? I did ask. And God did what I asked."

"What did you ask?"

"I asked Him to make you come back. And He did—as soon as I asked."

"You weren't afraid, were you?"

"I was too mad to be very afraid!"

"What happened?" She saw him grin.

"It wasn't funny. It's that Sarah! She was downright rude."

"Tell me about it."

Carla held out her thumb. "What do you make of this? Did you ever see it before?"

Marc took the ring off, stepped to the lamp and held it close to the light.

"Looks like a lodge ring of some sort. I've never seen one like it.

Where did you get it?"

"I found it."

Carla's words tumbled over each other as she told how she had gone to Matilda's room in search of the family jewels.

"I hope you didn't mind, Marc. It was done on impulse. You see, I've heard wealthy families always possess heirlooms—but I hadn't seen any."

Without waiting for a comment, she told of the stacks of shoes, and the discovery of the chest and the man's ring that seemed out of place in a drawer of pearls.

"And, just as I was about to put the ring back, Sarah sneaked in and snatched the chest from me."

"Sarah has a deep family loyalty," said Marc.

"That may be—but, did she have to be so rude?"

"I want to have a talk with them again before we leave. First, look at this." He opened a bank book.

"These are withdrawals. Thousands of dollars—over a period of less than two months. See, the last entry was dated May thirtieth—just four days before Aunt Matilda's death on June third. All withdrawals were paid in cash—authorized by her own signature. Just look at the last one—eighteen thousand dollars— and a zero balance."

"That's terrilbe. Do you think Ronald Powell got it all? How can the Kerneys help?"

"They might remember something they haven't told us. I've got to find that man!" Carla saw the muscles in his jaw ripple.

"Lead on, Mr. Holmes. I'm right behind you."

He grabbed her hand and, at the Kerneys' door, he rapped sharply. Sarah peeked out. She acted nervous, avoiding Carla's eyes.

"I'd like another talk with you and Walt," said Marc. She opened the door and motioned them in.

"I'll get Walt. He's jes' outside."

Marc was terse. "I have to know more about this man, Powell." Walt came in, his hat clutched in his hand.

"Walt, do you know something you haven't told me about Aunt Matilda's visitor? Can you describe him?"

Walt ran his grimy hand through his hair. "Never seen his face that I remember."

"Neither did I," chirped Sarah. "He was allus hidin' behind somethin'."

"She's right. Times I was workin' the rose garden , he'd drive up in that big Cadillac, an' he'd wait 'til I turned my back 'fore he'd git out. One time I almost seen him, but, quick as a flash, he put his newspaper in front o' his face. But, he couldn't hide that shock o' white hair."

"How old would you say he is? Sixty?" asked Marc.

"Ever' bit o' that," nodded Walt.

"Well, I'd say he could'a been a lot younger, too," said Sarah. "He was tall and straight and quick movin'."

"Yeah, an' quite the ladies' man." Walt winked.

Sarah snorted, "Ya might as well tell him 'bout that las' night, Walt."

Walt paled. "If you're sure we won't git in trouble."

"Tell us, Walt," said Marc.

He sighed. "'Twas purty late. Me an' Sarah was tired and sleepy. They'd finished their dinner a long time ago. We could hear the stereo playin' loud—one o' them slow pieces. She wanted to take a peek." Walt pointed his thumb at Sarah.

"I didn't think we should, but I went along with her. We opened the door a crack and could see through the dining room clean to the entrance hall."

Sarah interrupted. "An' we couldn't believe what we seen. They was a-dancin' fit to kill—and that aunt of your'n you wouldn't 'a knowed her. Dressed in that weddin' dress o' hers an' them sassy shoes with the sparkly buckles."

"Why didn't you tell us this before?" Marc frowned. "Did you tell the police?"

"We was 'fraid to," said Sarah. "Jes' like I was 'fraid to tell 'em 'bout the letter I took from his suitcase."

"Yeah, an' Miss 'Tilda would'a fired us for spyin'."

Marc took Carla's arm. "Thanks a lot for your help."

Away from the Kerneys' apartment, Carla blurted, "You see, she did have on the wedding dress—and she did use the violet perfume that night."

"Just a minute." Marc dashed back to the apartment. Without

72

knocking, he opened the door and stuck his head in. "Sarah, I'll take care of the jewel chest now."

"Oh, sure, Mr. Randall," she stammered, and in a moment, handed the box to him. "I was takin' care of it for ya."

Back in the living room, Marc said, "Let me have another look at that ring." He slipped it from her thumb and held it under the lamp. "It's a strange symbol. Wonder what it stands for?"

Carla shuddered. "It's hideous. Looks like that arrow goes through the ram's head, and the ruby is supposed to be a drop of blood, I'm sure."

"Get your bag. We'll stop by the bank in Central City and leave the jewels in the vault. You can take care of the ring. It could be an important clue."

When they finished their errand at the bank, they headed for Idaho Springs. As they reached Grant's Haven, Marc said, "I'll pick you up at seven. Tonight we go to Fredrick's."

Carla laughed. "Thanks for telling me. The appropriate dress for Fredrick's isn't jeans and sneakers."

9

It's about time I get to see my daughter." Patricia Brinks kissed Carla's cheek.

"Hi, Mother. I'm sorry I didn't get back sooner. Did you have a good time at Willow Brook?"

"It was nice to see Norma again, but I'm always glad to get back home."

In the back bedroom Carla kicked off her shoes and stretched out on the bed. Her mother sat beside her and smoothed her brow.

"You look tired, honey. Why don't you take a little nap before dinner?"

"I don't have time. Did Irene tell you about my new man? Oh, you'll approve of him. He's very religious."

"Carla, dear, that reminds me—that book I gave you for your birthday—I'd rather you wouldn't read it. It's misleading, dear. The Bible is your best guide."

"Don't tell me you believe all that stuff about 'Hell, fire and brimstone'?"

At her mother's pained look, Carla put her arm around her. "I'm sorry, Mother dear, but it seems to me everybody is trying to tell me how to live my life."

"We're just interested in your welfare, Carla."

"You don't need to worry about me, Mother. I'm changing." She hadn't had a drink or a cigarette since she met Marc—and Jim hadn't crossed her mind for two whole days.

"I'm convinced the only sure way to change is to meet the right man." Carla laughed as she grabbed her robe and headed for the shower.

Well, she'd met the right man, and tonight at Fredrick's she planned to dazzle him into a confession of love for her. He just thought he liked his women casual. Wait 'til he feasted his eyes on her new low-cut, royal-blue number that clung to her like a fragrance!

Hours later, Carla Preston closed the door behind Marc, shrugged her shoulders, and tiptoed past her mother, who was alseep on the couch.

Carla hung the royal-blue number on a hanger and shook her head—he evidently still liked his women casual!

The evening at Fredrick's had been a dismal flop. From the very beginning, Marc seemed preoccupied and on guard. Her attempt at cleverness fell flat, and she'd never struggled so hard to keep a conversation alive. The six-course dinner was interminable.

It wasn't all Marc's fault, she thought, as she snuggled down in bed. She'd put up a barrier of her own against his power to hurt her. What was that power—something that was able to stem the tide of his emotions.

Carla awakened some time later, gasping for breath. Hands clamped over her mouth, body rigid, eyes staring into darkness, she knew why—the nightmare was still vivid in her mind. The same skyscrapers, flickering lights, that beckoning figure barely visible in the dense fog—always just out of reach—swept up a long flight of stairs, then vanished at the top landing.

Wide awake now, Carla noted this was the first time she'd had the nightmare since she'd met Marc. Why tonight? Was Marc slipping out of her life? She couldn't bear the thought. Sobs rocked her body.

Finally, in control of herself, she gave up the thought of sleep, put on her robe and shuffled to the kitchen. A sliver of light under the door was a comfort. She tapped gently, then peeked in. "Don't you two ever go to bed?"

"Join the club—take a look at your baby sister."

Irene's eyes were red and swollen.

"What's wrong?" Carla put her arms around her sister.

"Nothing's wrong!" Irene held her glass on the table with both hands, her face just over it. "My husband criticizes me, my mother's ashamed of me, my sister ignores me!"

Carla lifted the glass from Irene's hands and put it on the drainboard. "Come, Irene, let's go to bed."

"You don't have to help me. I can manage by myself!"

After Carla coaxed her along, Irene was finally ready for bed.

"Sis, will you help me remember we're s'posed to go to church with Mother tomorrow morning? I promised we'd both go."

Without answering, Carla switched off the light, and went back to the kitchen to see George.

"Thanks for taking her off my hands, Sis." George looked grim. "Have a little nightcap with me. I need a drinking partner."

"I don't like it anymore, George."

"Don't tell me you've gone religious."

Carla threw up her hands. "Heaven forbid! There are enough fanatics in this family already!"

As she thought of Marc and the disappointment of the evening, and the recurrence of the nightmare, she said, "On second thought, I will have that drink."

George smiled, poured a jigger of whiskey over ice cubes, and filled her glass with water.

"To better days—and nights." He lifted his glass.

"I'll drink to that." The old sneer twisted her mouth.

"Atta girl. You'll see, things are looking better all the time." He squeezed her hand. "I'll let you in on a little secret. I may get that Cadillac I want sooner than I thought."

"That's great. Business must be booming."

"Not bad, old girl, not bad. And I want you to know, you're welcome to stay with us as long as you want to."

"Thanks, George, but I've got to get back and sell my house again. Then I want to get away for good."

"I wonder if it'd help Irene to get away from here for awhile?"

"She's getting worse, isn't she? Do you think she's an alcoholic?"

"She drinks all day, every day—what would you think? Try to get her to go home with you, will you?" He poured two more drinks. "But—it may not be good to have her around Penny."

"Penny's lived with me long enough, nothing shocks her anymore." Carla gulped her drink and let George light her cigarette. She took a deep drag and closed her eyes.

"Did I tell you about my blackout? It happened the night of my birthday, after you and Irene went home. Penny helped me to bed."

She put her hand over her eyes. She really did miss Penny.

76

How would she be able to cope when Penny was married and on her own?

Then, I'll be really alone, Carla thought.

"There, there, Sis. Don't cry." He had come behind her and put his arms around her. His head rested on top of hers.

"I can't stand to see you hurt. I've really grown fond of you in the years Irene and I have been married."

"It must be the drink George. I always get sentimental." She slapped his arm, got up, and put her glass in the sink. "I'll get Irene to go home with me."

At the door she turned, "Mother wants us to go to church with her in the morning. Maybe you should come along, too."

"No, no—not me. Religion's for women and children."

Carla got in bed again, this time dizzy and disgusted. Why had she had those drinks with George? She hadn't really wanted them. Didn't she have any self-control at all? She was right back where she had started. Where were all those good intentions to regain her self-respect?

Before she realized it, she stood in the hall, telephone in her hand, waiting for Marc to answer.

"Is that you, Marc?"

"Carla, what's wrong? Where are you?"

"I had to hear your voice, Marc. Don't come over. I just had a couple of drinks with George. I'm sorry."

She hung up before he could say anything more. Oh, what would he think of her? She'd probably never see him again.

She went back to the kitchen. George was gone. She sat at the table, her head in her hands, staring straight ahead. She couldn't go back to bed. The nightmare would surely come again. Should she have another drink? Alone? She shivered in the cold—better go get into her slippers.

As she stepped inside the bedroom, she stopped and listened, every thought hushed. There it was again—unmistakable tapping on the window.

Her light was on. They'd know someone was awake. To keep her shadow from showing on the filmy drapes, she crawled to the lamp beside her bed and switched it off. She peeked out. The figure of a man, silhouetted by the patio light, stood close to the half-open window.

Before she could scream, he called, "Little Peanut."

"Marc," she gasped, "what are you doing out there?"

"Serenading my love. Get dressed. I'll meet you at the kitchen door."

Carla's heart sang as she stepped into a jumpsuit, scribbled a note for Irene, opened the back door and fell into his arms.

"My Little Peanut. You had me worried."

"I'm all right now, Marc darling."

Driving down the highway, Marc kept up a continuous flow of conversation. She was aware of his motive. He wanted her to forget about George and the drinks.

He spoke of the many night noises: shadows, grotesque and playful, made by overhanging branches . . . the mysterious blue of the night sky over the mountain peaks . . .

Then in picturesque speech, he talked about her. "Your hair is like thistledown, tinted with Indian Paintbrush . . . your eyes, the blue glacier lakes in summer . . . your lips are sweet, wild strawberries . . ."

Carla stored the rythm of his words in her heart, afraid to breathe lest the poetic flow stop.

In a slight change of meter, she knew his eyes twinkled as he mentioned the lightness of her step . . . the ripple of her laugh . . . the joy of her presence.

After each pause, she waited—yet, waited in vain—for the words, "I love you."

Content for the present with these rapturous moments, she nestled against his shoulder, acutely aware of the smoothness of his chin on her forehead and the fragrance of after-shave.

Roused by tires crunching gravel, she looked out at the small roadside inn. "Where are we?"

"Just outside Georgetown. How about a snack?"

In the quaint German inn a small three-piece orchestra played a polka. There were two couples at the edge of the small dance floor. Marc chose a table in the corner of the room.

"Three o'clock! No wonder I'm hungry," said Carla.

After the buxom waitress in a dirndl dress and tri-cornered scarf took their order, Marc lifted Carla's hands to his lips.

He kissed her finger tips, and in a husky voice he said, "I steeled myself against you all evening at Fredrick's. You were like a song—too beautiful for the spoken word."

Suddenly his hands tightened. She followed his gaze to a table near them. Clearly audible from where they sat, one of the men said, "Did they ever get the guy that swindled old lady Lovelace?"

His words had an immediate reaction on Marc. He leaped to their table and in a tight, controlled voice Carla heard him say, "Pardon me. I couldn't help overhearing what you just said. The man you spoke of . . ." He pulled a chair up to their table.

"I'm an insurance investigator. What can you tell me about him? I believe this might be the man I'm looking for."

Marc gave one of his business cards to the man. "Could you give me a description of him?"

They all shook their heads. One of the ladies spoke up. "They say no one ever saw his face. It's really a weird case."

"We all know he was here in Georgetown," said the man. "Especially old Miss Lucy Lovelace. She'd be able to describe him, I'm sure."

Marc got her address from them and came back to Carla. "Tomorrow we'll call on Miss Lucy Lovelace."

"Oh, I can't go with you. Irene promised Mother we'd both go to church with her." Carla grimaced.

"Great!" Marc's raised eyebrow registered surprise. "I'll pick you up for church, then we'll go to the Lovelace place after lunch."

10

It was Sunday morning, July sixth. At ten forty-five sharp the doorbell rang. Carla let Marc in and introduced him to her mother while two blocks away, church bells accompanied the singing of her heart.

"Let's walk to church," said Mrs. Brinks. "It's good exercise."

"And a good suggestion," Marc beamed at her and tucked Carla's hand under his arm.

They strolled down the quiet, tree-lined street, leaf patterns dancing before them on the cracked sidewalk.

Marc looked at Carla's upturned face. "Your eyes are like violets dipped in dew."

Her eyelids fluttered. "Such poetry—and so early in the morning, too."

Her pulses throbbed with the beauty of the morning and the pleasure of being near Marc.

In the foyer of the little church, weighted with guilt, Carla remembered she hadn't been to church since Penny was a little girl.

Bitterness still clung to her as she moved down the aisle, recalling the events of that long-ago Sunday morning. She had taken Penny to Sunday School for the first time, explaining to Herb that their child should have some religious training. When they got back home, Herb sat in his favorite chair, a Bible propped up in front of him.

Without a word of greeting, he said in his high-pitched voice, "Have you ever read this thing? No wonder it's a best seller! It's the sexiest book on the market!"

His remark had shocked Carla. Though she'd never read the Bible, she'd been taught to respect it. She'd never gone to church again.

Carla followed her mother and Irene down the aisle. Everybody shook hands with everybody. Marc acted like he'd known these people all his life. Why did they have to go so far down to the front? The benches were hard and slippery. Sandwiched between Irene and Marc, her white linen suit would be ruined, she thought with irritation.

If she looked straight ahead, she wouldn't have to speak to anyone. They were so close to the front she could read the inscription on the table in front of the pulpit. "This Do in Remembrance of Me." Do what? She could do a much better job of flower arranging.

She counted the people in the choir. Five men and six women—black robes, white collars. Why did their faces shine? And they looked happy—like they were expecting something great. Carla glanced across the aisle—the same eager intensity.

There seemed to be a lot of noise. She thought it was supposed to be quiet and reverent in church. That young mother at the end of the row kept wrestling with her little boy. What a loud noise those hard-soled shoes made thumping the wooden bench! The teenage section was a wave of activity. Chewing gum and passing notes, titters and giggles—why didn't someone put a stop to it?

Her attention was brought back to the front. A short, pudgy man stepped behind the pulpit and raised his hands high over his head—a signal for everybody to stand.

After they sang, "Praise God From Whom All Blessings Flow," there was more scuffling as everybody shook hands again. Marc stepped across the aisle and shook hands with a woman he didn't know.

When things quieted down, a young blonde girl came down from the choir loft to the pulpit and sang. Her voice was sweet, but the song was so sad. The words were about Jesus dying on the cross all alone.

As soon as she sat down, the preacher took his place behind the pulpit, held on to the sides, and closed his eyes. The red-haired lady at the organ played softly while the preacher prayed. How could he memorize such a long prayer?

When he said "Amen," the organ boomed out louder, and two men passed wooden plates down the rows of benches. Why did Marc put a twenty-dollar bill in it? Wasn't that a little heavy?

After all the preliminaries, the preacher stepped to the pulpit again. He couldn't be more than twenty-five, and certainly not very good-looking with that thin, sandy hair, and those horn-rimmed glasses that were too big for his narrow face. Suddenly, his voice boomed with vibrance.

He said something about "the lost," and looked right at her. His words, sober and strange, went on and on. Jesus was God. He was coming back to earth in His own body. It could be today. He would set up His kingdom here on earth.

Carla tried to close her ears when he spoke of Hell as a literal place and the devil as a real person. He told her if she didn't receive the gift of God's Son, she'd go to Hell.

"Heaven or Hell. Where are you going, my friend?"

Carla looked at her crumpled bulletin. The heat in the small room was unbearable. Why didn't someone open the windows?

Irene nudged her. "Do you think we should go down front?" she whispered.

"Are you crazy? I'm not gonna make a fool of myself!"

"Come today. Come as you are. Tomorrow may be too late." The preacher pleaded.

Carla bored herself into the bench. Marc's eyes were closed—praying again, no doubt.

What was Irene doing? She stepped in front of them, and she and their mother made their way to the front of the church. Marc touched Irene's shoulder as she passed by. Her mother was smiling and crying.

There was whispering between the preacher and Irene; then, his face radiant, he announced to the congregation, "This young lady has just made a decision for Jesus Christ."

Carla's throat was dry. Why did she feel deserted? Irene hadn't left her. She had probably done the right thing. She needed help with her drinking.

What was Marc thinking? She wouldn't look at him. If he even so much as hinted that she should do that—well, that would be the end of their friendship, right now.

As they neared home, Carla's mother asked Marc to stay for dinner.

"Thank you, I'd like that," he said.

George was waiting on the porch when they got home. Irene ran to him, threw her arms around his neck and kissed him. He looked suspicious.

"What gives?" he said.

"I'm a new person, George. I went forward in church this morning and received Jesus as my Saviour."

"Really?" George nodded at Marc. "It's good to see you."

In a few minutes Mrs. Brinks called from the kitchen, "Find a place at the table; dinner's ready."

The meal was pleasant, conversation general. After dessert, Mrs. Brinks shocked Carla with, "How long have you been a Christian, Marc?" Didn't she know that was a personal thing?

Marc answered her enthusiastically. "I received Christ when I was a teenager. I confess I didn't live for Him 'til about two years ago. I went to an evangelistic meeting and dedicated my life to the Lord. I've been a lot happier since then."

"Just what does that mean?" asked George. "You say you dedicated your life. Are you gonna be a preacher?"

Marc laughed. "Not necessarily. In fact, I can't see myself as a preacher. I don't know what the Lord has in mind for me yet. But when I find out, I'll be willing to do it."

Carla didn't want to seem too interested. "How will you know what He wants you to do? Will you have a dream or hear voices, or what?"

"He speaks in different ways to different people. I believe He'll put His desires in my mind—and I'll think that's exactly what I wanted all along."

He looked flustered for the first time since Carla had met him. "I don't know how else to explain it, but I'm sure the Lord will make it clear to me."

"No doubt about it." Carla couldn't help the note of sarcasm.

"And what about Irene and Mom Brinks, here?" said George. "Will He send them off to the mission fields?"

He and Carla laughed too loudly.

Marc pushed his chair back. "Thank you for that good home-cooked meal, Mrs. Brinks. Now, if you'll excuse us, we have some business in Georgetown."

"Run along, you two," said Irene. "Have fun. If you get back in time, we can go to the evening service."

On the way to Georgetown, Carla was glad Marc made no

reference to Irene's decision—wasn't that what they had called it?

Traffic was heavy on the main street. Marc assumed the air of a tourist guide once more.

"Georgetown, the Queenly City of the West, is experiencing its greatest boom in years."

Carla laughed. "I suppose you know its complete history, too. Do continue."

"You asked for it. Georgetown was named the 'Queenly City' because it is distinct from all other Colorado cities, culturally speaking. For example, the Watson House, one of the luxury homes, has been preserved in every detail. There you'll see just a glimpse of the culture brought into the Old West from all parts of the world. We'll take a look at it when we finish our business."

"A visit to the home of Lucy Lovelace, I assume," said Carla.

"Precisely. Our purpose: to get an accurate description of the elusive Ronald Powell."

"And to uncover the mystery of the strange ring."

Marc took a handkerchief from his hip pocket and gave it to her. She unfolded it and slipped the ring on her thumb. "It's so gruesome," she shuddered. "What kind of lodge would use such a symbol?"

"If we knew that, we'd be able to trace some of its members."

"Ronald Powell must be a member. But how can we know that's his real name? And what does he look like?"

Marc pulled to a stop in front of a neat, two-story frame house. "We should know in a few minutes," he said.

Carla looked down the street, wider than most found in small mountain towns. The lawns on both sides were like short shag carpets, the sidewalks like white satin ribbons. Every house wore fresh white paint, their individuality displayed in various color trims.

A middle-aged woman stood in the doorway of the two-story house. "You lookin' for Miss Lovelace?"

"Yes, we are," said Marc. "May we see her?"

"I'll find out if it's all right." She motioned to them. "You can come on in, if you like."

Ushered into the presence of Lucy Lovelace, Carla stared at the tall, straight, handsome woman. Eighty years old? Impossible.

She asked them to sit down. Marc was businesslike, yet gentle.

"We need a description of Ronald Powell, Miss Lovelace. We have been informed you'd be able to supply it."

Calmly, she said he was a little above average height, straight, medium build. She thought his eyes were blue. His hair was thick and white.

"But it wasn't his looks alone that attracted me," smiled Miss Lovelace. "It was his elegant manners. Charming, complimentary—seemed to know just what to say to make a woman feel beautiful and loved." She looked down at her folded hands.

Marc raise his eyebrows at Carla. To Miss Lovelace, he said, "Dear lady, do you think you could be a little more specific? What kind of car did he drive, for instance?"

"It was a big one," she said. "Shiny black."

"How did he dress? Were his clothes expensive-looking?"

"Indeed, yes. He always looked like he stepped right out of a fashion magazine."

"Do you remember if he wore jewelry of any kind?" Marc took the ring from Carla's thumb. "Have you ever seen this before?"

Lucy Lovelace turned pale as she held it in her hand.

"He said he'd never part with it. Where did you get it? Has something happened to him?"

Marc took the ring from her. "Thank you for your help, Miss Lovelace."

"Let me tell you this, young man." Her eyes flashed. "I don't regret anything. I gained more than I lost. And, you might as well know, I won't prefer charges against him."

"Ronald Powell must be quite a lover boy," said Carla. They both laughed as they got in the car.

"The day is still young," said Marc. "We'll go through Watson House, then I want to check something at Winthrop House before we go back to Idaho Springs. Do you want to go to the evening service?"

"No, thanks," Carla stiffened.

When they stopped in front of a place called Alpine Lodge, Marc explained, "This is it. The original structure of the fabulous

Watson House."

In the small reception hall, Carla stopped next to a document on the wall.

"Look, Marc, this tells all about Watson House. It cost only four thousand five hundred, originally. William A. Hamill had it remodeled. It was one of the most luxurious homes in the state, it says here."

Marc laughed. "Now you sound like a tour guide. Read further. It says there were mirrors made of diamond dust, and wallpaper flocked with gold, silver and camel's hair."

"I can hardly wait to see it all!" Carla took his arm and pushed him along.

Later, Carla said, "That was an hour well spent. I wouldn't have missed it for anything."

They were on a narrow, winding road, climbing steadily. Carla clung to Marc's arm. "Where are we going?"

"This is a shortcut I discovered a long time ago. It takes less than fifteen minutes from here to Winthrop House. I've timed it." He was like a young boy ready to reveal a secret.

Carla's eyes were glued to the road, her muscles tense at every sharp curve. She sighed with relief at the turn into the circular driveway of Winthrop House.

Hand in hand they bounded up the steps. Marc stopped short, and in a protective gesture, swept her behind him. The front door stood ajar. He pushed it open, looked in on both sides, then drew her in.

"Looks like we've had a visitor. It's a good thing we stopped by."

"I hope they aren't still here." Carla shivered.

"Do you want to come with me and have a look around?"

"Of course. Do you think I want to stay here by myself?"

"Come then, Watson, old fellow. Brace yourself. We'll check the Kerneys' apartment first. They aren't here on Sundays."

With her hand tucked under his arm, Carla had to run to keep up as he strode across the wide room to the small door that led to the kitchen.

Inside, at the far end of the kitchen, the curtains rippled. Carla's breath caught in her throat, Marc's arm flexed.

"What are your deductions, Dr. Watson?"

"A possible breeze from an open window, wouldn't you say, Holmes?" Carla clung to Marc, fighting hysteria.

"We'll take it slow. Do you see that dirt on the floor by the window?"

"I'm way ahead of you," said Carla. "The intruder came in this way, and left through the front door."

"Elucidate, my good man."

"The dirt was brought in on his shoes picked up from the flower bed outside the window. If he had come in the front door, the dirt would have been left back there."

"Excellent deduction, Dr. Watson."

Inside the Kerneys' apartment, Carla stood with her back to the door while Marc made a quick check of the rest of the apartment. Without wasting time, he whisked her out, and on up the stairs to Matilda's room.

The door was closed, but deep scars on the facing showed it had been forced. Inside, the lovely room was in a shambles. Carla wanted to scream with rage, or cry with pain at the sight of all Matilda's elegant gowns in a jumbled heap on the floor. Shoe boxes were emptied on the bed, drawers turned upside down on the floor.

"Who could have done this?" Marc's eyes flashed.

"What were they looking for?" Carla moaned. In a daze, she pulled the wedding gown from the mass and hung it on a hanger. Marc put his arm about her waist and led her out.

Back in the car, he said, "We'll stop in Central City and report this to the police. There's enough new evidence to reopen the investigation."

11

On the way back to Idaho Springs, Marc seemed pre-occupied. The captain at police headquarters in Central City was cooperative and assured Marc they would investigate the forced entry complaint the following day. He said it would be necessary for Marc and Carla to be on hand when they arrived at Winthrop House.

Irene met Carla at the door, her eyes wide. "Jim's here—in room four. Had too much to drink, wants to see you."

"We'll go right over." Marc grabbed Carla's arm and stalked off the porch.

"Don't, Marc. He said he'd like to kill you."

Heedless of the warning, Marc headed for the motel. At room four, Carla tapped, then called Jim's name.

The door flew open. Jim Frazer swayed as he tried to focus his eyes. "What's *he* doing here?" He pointed at Marc.

"I want to hear what you have to say, Jim."

Unceremoniously, Jim jerked Carla into the room and shoved her toward the bed. She caught herself in time to see Marc close the door and lean against it. She was surprised to hear his voice of authority.

"Now, what did you have to say?"

Jim rubbed his hands through his hair and staggered backward, giving Marc an opportunity to leap to Carla's side.

Jim's eyes seemed to plead with Carla. "You didn't tell me you were staying up here so long, honey. I couldn't get you at your house or the shop. Then, I just happened to see Penny on the street and she told me you were still up here. I came as fast as I could get away. I want you to come back."

What would Marc think? Carla was speechless.

"It's all your fault." Jim started toward Marc. "I don't like you one little bit. I want my woman back." He turned from Marc and lunged at Carla.

Marc grabbed one of his arms and brought it up in a hammer lock. Jim groaned and stared at Carla. The quick action startled her, too. Jim was no match for Marc's powerful arms and shoulders.

"Listen to me, Jim." The same power sounded in his low voice. "Carla doesn't have to account to you for anything. It should be clear to you she no longer wants your attention."

Jim, still in pain, mumbled, "Who do you think you are? I'll see her 'til she tells me not to."

Carla came closer, her throat so dry she could hardly make herself heard.

"Jim, please listen. I'm telling you now. I don't want to see you again."

Jim rubbed his shoulder as Marc released his hold.

"You'll hear from me again," he threatened. "You promised to marry me when Sue divorces me."

Carla raced ahead of Marc, her face burning with humiliation. Before she got to the kitchen door, Marc caught her in his arms. She sobbed against his chest. "I'm sorry, Marc. What can I say?"

"Don't say anything," he whispered in her hair. "I'll be at the hotel if you need me."

She threw her arms around his neck. "Oh, Marc, I do need you—but, I'm not . . ."

"Carla, listen to me. We won't talk of the past again. Now and the future are ours to . . ." He tilted her chin and looked at her tenderly. "I'll see you in the morning. Goodnight, Little Peanut."

She watched him turn the corner of the house, then tapped on the kitchen window. Irene opened the door a crack.

"Oh, Sis, I was so worried. What happened?"

"It was pretty awful. I'm so ashamed. I feel like the notorious scarlet woman." She dropped into a chair, her head in her hands. "Jim let Marc know, in no uncertain terms . . ."

"How embarrassing! I'm sorry, Sis. What did Marc do?"

"He was wonderful. Told Jim to leave me alone. They even fought over me." She smiled bitterly.

"Did they hit each other?"

"No. Marc just held Jim away from me. Jim was drunk. Marc knew how to handle him."

"How did you get into such a mess with Jim in the first place?"

"Who knows? Lonely, I guess. I knew he was married but I

guess I just didn't care. I believed him and was sorry for him when he told me his wife didn't understand him."

"Do you think he'll try to see you again?"

"I know he will. The question is—will I let him?"

The hopeless future weighed her down. "Why don't you come home with me, Irene? I need your moral support. Besides, you said you'd help with Penny's bridesmaids' dresses."

Irene smiled. "George would probably be glad to be rid of me. He's acted so strange all day. Tiptoes around and sort of whispers to me like I'm from the spirit world. Do I look different to you?"

"You look sober—and you look pretty, too." Carla saw a change in her sister's mouth and eyes.

"I can't explain how I feel," Irene bubbled. "I've never known such peace and joy—and love, real love for everybody."

Carla studied her sister's face. After a moment, she said, "Someday, I might—but not now, too busy . . ."

In the bedroom, loneliness overwhelmed her. She felt that invisible wall—the same wall that stood between her and Penny, then—her mother—and Marc—and now, it was rising between her and Irene. It was as real as the nightmare, yet more tangible and frightening.

Sunlight streamed through the parted drapes as Carla lay still, searching her mind for a semblance of the nightmare. The muscles in her neck relaxed. Last night she was sure her sleep would be interrupted by the rising wall, along with the nightmare.

Marc had said to forget the past—impossible as long as the wall remained between them. Before she and Marc could share any part of the future, the wall had to be dealt with. Today she'd come right out and ask him if he felt it too.

The thought of seeing him in a few minutes stirred her into action. In jeans, faded shirt and sneakers—his own choice for the casual woman—she poured a glass of orange juice and started the coffee. There was a light tap at the back door. "I didn't want to disturb anyone," he whispered, taking her in his arms.

Her senses reeled at the scent of shaving lotion and touch of his smooth-shaven chin resting on her forehead.

Later, approaching Winthrop House, Walt Kerney could be seen bending over the roses. He peered from under his straw hat, then immediately disappeared behind the house.

"Why is Walt so sneaky?" Carla asked as they got out of the car. "Do you think he's hiding something?"

"I don't know if he is or not," Marc laughed. "You make a fine detective. Suspicious of everyone, aren't you?"

"You don't trust the Kerneys any more than I do." She searched his eyes. "Do you?"

"No comment, yet."

Inside, Marc lit the logs in the fireplace and pulled the long silk cord. Carla's eyes fastened on the small door. Almost instantly Sarah swooped into the room. Again, her beady eyes bored through Carla and her thin lips formed an arc of disapproval.

In a few words Marc told her why they had come so early. Sarah was visibly shaken by the news of an intruder.

"Who could it 'a been?" she screeched.

"The police will find out. They should be here any minute now. First, I want you to see Miss Matilda's room."

The doorbell rang at the same time they reached the landing. Marc unlocked the bedroom door. "That's the police," he said. "I'll bring them up. You can wait in there."

The minute they were left alone, Sarah came close to Carla, and in a voice low and menacing, she said, "I know your type. Tryin' to worm your way into the Winthrop fortune, ain't ya? Well, I'm warnin' ya. It won't work."

Carla reeled under the accusation. Sarah stepped to the window. Hatred in her eyes slashed the distance between them.

Then Marc came in, followed by two policemen. When Sarah started to pick up some of the scattered clothes, one of the men shouted at her, "Don't touch anything." Sarah backed away, eyes wide.

Marc stepped to her side. "You remember Sarah Kerney, Officer. You've questioned her before. And this is Mrs. Preston, my assistant."

"You still working on this case, Mr. Randall?"

"Yes, we are." His eyes included Carla.

"Well, I'd say, with this forced entry and Miss Winthrop's room

91

the evident target of the search, there's sufficient reason to continue a more active investigation."

After taking a few notes, he said, "Now, we'd like a review of the events on the night preceding the death and the discovery of the body the next morning, in detail."

"Mrs. Kerney is able to give you that information." Marc led Carla to the window seat and motioned the men to chairs.

A wave of pity swept over Carla for the birdlike woman who stood in the center of the room, all color drained from her face.

Without compassion, the questioning began, one asking, the other taking notes.

"We'll start with the evening before she died. In your statement before, you said Miss Winthrop had company for dinner that night. Give us the names of the guests and the details of the evening."

"They was only one guest, I told ya before." Her eyes flashed. " 'Twas that man Ronald Powell. Miss 'Tilda said it was a farewell dinner party for him. She wanted it jes' right."

"I believe you told us before you'd never seen Ronald Powell's face. How do you know it was him?"

"All that white hair, o'course. An' I heard her call him Ronald."

"Proceed with the details."

"Well, the two of 'em was dressed fit to kill." Sarah clamped her hand over her mouth. "If ya'll forgive the expression, Mr. Randall."

"Go on," the officer prodded. "What time was the dinner over?"

"They was still at the table at ten o'clock. 'Course they wasn't eatin' all that time." Sarah's nose twitched.

"Lollygaggin', they was—beg pardon Mr. Randall—but your aunt was a silly old fool, if ya ask me."

"What time did Ronald Powell leave?" the officer continued, tonelessly.

"I don't know. Me and Walt went to bed 'bout 'leven." Sarah looked at Marc, "Should I tell 'em what we seen?"

"Of course, Sarah. They need every scrap of information we can give them."

"Well, Walt woke me up—I don't know what time it was. He told me to come see somethin' he thought was funny. I went with

92

him to the dining room door and we both peeked in. We could see clean through to the entrance hall, where the floor is slippery. They was a-dancin'. The music was loud, but real slow. He'd put his face to her ear like he was whisperin', then she'd throw back her head and laugh. I don't know where she got all that pep, at her age."

"Was that the last time you saw her alive?"

Carla shuddered at his bluntness. Sarah seemed at a loss. "I guess 'twas. I thought she was alive when I seen her the next mornin', but she warn't."

"Start with the next morning."

"I always brought breakfast to her in bed at eight o'clock sharp. That's the way she wanted it. That mornin', I wasn't sure since she was up 'til I don't know when."

"Tell us the exact position of the body when you first saw it that morning."

"I already told ya a hundred times."

"Tell us a hundred and one times."

"Like I said 'fore, she was so natural-lookin', she looked unnatural. Flat on her back, her head straight on the pillow, not a hair out o' place, hands on the outside of the covers, palms up, peaceful-like, legs stretched out straight."

"You said you didn't know she was dead at first. When did you discover that fact?"

"I called her. She didn't answer. I put the tray on the table by her bed. Then, I pulled the drapes to let the sunshine in. She liked it that way. I went back and called her again. I watched her close. She didn't move. I touched her arm. It was—hard as a rock."

Sarah stood motionless, rigid.

"What did you do then?" The officer touched her arm. Sarah's scream crescendoed. Marc took her in his arms and smoothed her hair.

"There, there, dear Sarah. It's all right. You've done your part. Go to Walt now." She stumbled out.

"This case is different from the others, Mr. Randall. Are you aware we've had similar cases of swindling? Your aunt, however, is the only dead victim."

Carla was furious. How could anyone be that callous?

"The other victims are unwilling to testify or bring charges against the suspected male, and have repeatedly stated they hope he will not be apprehended."

Marc signaled a warning to Carla. He wasn't going to mention Lucy Lovelace.

"What do you stand to gain by your aunt's death, Mr. Randall?"

Under apparent control, Marc said, "My mother would have been the sole beneficiary, but it was decided between the two sisters, long before Aunt Matilda's death, that the estate would be left to me, with the stipulation I would be responsible for the preservation of Winthrop House and its original beauty."

"Do you plan to live here then?"

"As soon as the estate is settled, I plan to open a law office in Central City. I can keep an eye on the place from there." So, he was a lawyer, too. Carla was proud of him.

On his way out, the officer spokesman said, "Since this new angle of forced entry has come up, there will probably be a delay in settlement. Do you have any idea what the intruder was looking for?"

"Not off hand." There was another signal between them.

When they were alone, Marc said, "We'd better put that ring in the vault. You still have it, don't you?"

"Did you give it back to me after you showed it to Lucy Lovelace?"

He shook his head. "My memory is a blank. I know I looked for it in my other pants pocket this morning before I left. It wasn't there, so I thought I gave it back to you. It's probably in your purse."

"Not this one. It would have to be in the one I carried to church."

"Well, it's no immediate problem. But, if that's what the intruder was looking for, it must be important."

Carla shivered. She put her arm through his, and pressed her face against his shoulder.

"Marc, I still don't trust the Kerneys. I'm really afraid of Sarah."

12

"Little Peanut, don't be afraid. Just look into the fire and forget your fears." Carla nestled closer to Marc. She was beginning to feel comfortable in this huge room with its impressive fireplace.

"Are you my psychiatrist? How many talents have you, Mr. Randall? Doctor, lawyer, merchant . . ."

Marc tilted her chin. "We're not talking about me. Let me look at you."

She closed her eyes, waiting—always waiting. How she longed to feel his lips on hers, and to hear the words, "I love you." Moments like these always ended in silence—motionless silence. Slowly she opened her eyes. He was gazing at the smoldering logs. The ever-present wall rose higher.

"Is this your standard treatment for your mental patients?" she quipped, struggling for composure.

He stepped to the fireplace and stirred the logs, apparently seeking the right answer. Then he pushed a hassock to the couch and sat facing her. "Let's get back to the diagnosis. Do you mind talking about your fears?"

"All of them?" she asked, flippantly. "How much time do you have, Dr. Randall?"

"Be serious, Little Peanut. I know you're afraid of many things. Why don't you bring them out in the open and let's analyze them, one by one."

She drew her feet up on the couch and locked her arms about her knees. "Okay," she sighed, "you know I'm afraid of Sarah."

"Tell me why."

"She hates me. Up in Aunt Matilda's room today, before you came up with the police, she practically threatened me. Said I was trying to worm my way into the Winthrop fortune."

Marc frowned. "That's a new side of Sarah I haven't seen. I'll look into the underlying factors immediately. But, first, go on. What other fears do you have?"

"I'm desperately afraid of Mr. Cecil Barker. I won't bore you with the details."

"How can we analyze them if you keep anything from me?"

"They're personal reasons. I'll analyze them myself when I have more time."

"I'd like to help you, Carla."

"You know I'm afraid of Jim Frazer. He's terribly hot-tempered and jealous. But he'll get over it, I'm sure."

She got up and paced back and forth in front of him. "I'm afraid of ordinary things, like mountain driving, thunder and lightning, floods, earthquakes."

She talked of her fear of growing old and being alone, of sickness and pain, and—death. She folded her arms across her breast and faced him. This was a good time to tell him about the wall.

"And there's a nightmare. Always the same. It leaves me trembling and depressed—but, Marc there's a new fear that dwarfs all the others. There's a wall rising higher and higher all the time. I can't see over it or around it. You're on the other side—" She paused, then said, "Can you analyze it, doctor?"

Marc got up, placed his hands on her shoulders, and looked deep into her eyes. "I believe I can. Are you willing to listen?"

"It's tormenting me. Are you aware of it, too? I mean, do you feel a wall between us?" She pushed away from him. "I suppose it has something to do with religion, but I've got to know."

"Then, listen to me with an open mind and heart. I'll tell you what I think it is." He seemed to brace himself. This must be important to him.

"I believe the wall is your own will. As long as you fight against God's will for your life, you're building a wall between you and God."

"What is God's will for me? Can anyone know?"

"Only if you really want to know, and are willing to do what He directs."

Carla paced back and forth. "That's a big order. Oh, well, at least I know now what the wall is."

She stopped, threw her arms around his neck and pressed against him. "Marc, why can't you take me just as I am? Why must there be a wall between us? Between God and me—okay—but, between us, too?"

He slipped her arms from around his neck and held her hands in his. "I'm afraid so."

Growing anger released her pent-up emotions. "Just what do you want me to be? You've found fault with me from the beginning. It's impossible to meet your standards!" She put her hands on her hips.

"I'm me! Take me as I am or not at all. You can't make a Holy Joe out of me—no way!" She flounced to the front door. "As far as I'm concerned, it's over—right here and now!"

A heavy fog drifted over her mind. The nightmare was a vivid reality. Marc had slipped through her fingers—his shadow was walking away . . .

From time to time on the way back to Idaho Springs, she glanced at his relaxed hands on the steering wheel. She couldn't bring herself to look at his face. Not a word was said. Why didn't he talk to her? Why didn't he say she was all right the way she was? Didn't she mean anything to him after all? Her chest ached; her fingertips throbbed.

At her sister's front door, in a low and controlled voice, Marc spoke the first words since they had left Winthrop House.

"Carla, I want you to know, if you ever need me, Irene will have my phone number."

Her eyes darting over her shoulder, she snapped, "Don't count on it."

Hours later, his words still tormented her. If she needed him? He knew she needed him. But, he evidently didn't need her. She'd be glad when she got away from here. It was good that Irene was going home with her. She needed her stabilizing influence. So much to be done—Penny's wedding, the house to be sold—then what?

The next morning there was an air of excitement mingled with sadness as Carla said goodbye to her mother and George, and was on her way with Irene back to Englewood.

Determined to forget Marc and everything connected with

him—Winthrop House, Aunt Matilda, the mystery—Carla suddenly remembered she hadn't looked for the ring. She reached in the back seat for her white bag and went through it. There was nothing but a few facial tissues. How strange. She always kept her different bags well supplied with lipstick, comb, cologne, and always some mad-money.

"Irene, do me a favor. When you get back home, call Marc—he'll leave his number with you—and just tell him I don't have the ring."

"What ring?"

"He'll understand. That's all you need to say." Carla didn't want to talk about it. She had to forget Marc as soon as possible.

"I'll tell you all about it after we get home. Right now I have to think about other things, like selling my house."

"How do you expect to sell it? Isn't Mr. Barker still holding up the deal?"

"Probably. I guess the only way out is to marry him." The idea repulsed her.

"What about Marc? I thought you were crazy about him."

"I have to forget him. The sooner the better." She longed for him already. Why did she cling so doggedly to her independence?

One day ran into the other. Penny was all chatter. Irene worked with her on the bridesmaids' dresses during the day while Carla tried to be interested in her shop.

In the evenings, conversation centered on the wedding and always ended with the Bible. Completely out of it, Carla's anxieties increased with her diminishing bank balance.

After Irene went home, Carla called Cecil Barker. In her most provocative manner, she asked him to take her to dinner.

That evening, Mr. Barker openly displayed his delight to have her in his company again.

"My dear Carla, what an unexpected turn of events!" His small eyes flicked over her. "Still the charming, beautiful girl I've set my heart on."

During the evening, Carla was miserable with her continuous comparison of Mr. Barker and Marc. Constantly alert to keep his conversation on generalities instead of broaching the subject of marriage to her, she was exhausted by the time he took her home, and thoroughly convinced her problems could be solved another way.

At the door of her house, Cecil Barker stood too close to her. "Before I leave, my dear, may I bring up the subject of my last proposal?"

"Dear Mr. Barker, please don't rush me this time."

His small damp hand patted her cheek. "As you wish," he wheezed. "Goodnight, my dear."

Inside the door, Carla shuddered visibly.

"What's wrong, Mom?" Penny was still up.

"Nothing at all. Just a little tired, I guess."

"You're not happy, are you, Mom? Is it because I'm getting married?"

"Of course not, Kitten. How are things going? Is there anything I can do?" Carla longed to hear Penny say she needed her for something—anything.

"Everything's under control. Just think, only a week now. Ray's bringing my dress over on his lunch hour tomorrow. Wait'll you see it! You'll love it!"

"Is Ray working?"

"Just a temporary job 'til school starts in the fall. He's working in a florist shop. Just think, he'll be able to get all the flowers for the wedding at a discount. Isn't the Lord good?"

Carla stared at her without comment.

"Everything's working out just right. Ray's mom is getting her sister to help us get dressed at the church that night."

Carla felt light-headed.

"You're so busy, Mom. We thought you'd be relieved if you didn't have to do anything."

Carla backed into her bedroom and closed her door. In a hypnotic trance, she got ready for bed, barely conscious of the rumble of thunder in the distance.

Under the covers, she put her hands over her ears and drew her knees up to her chin. Marc's face materialized from the dull recesses of her mind. Oh, Marc, where are you? I need you.

Carla fought the impulse to go to the kitchen for a drink. She hadn't weakened since she had come back home. It had to be Marc's influence. Even the continual return of the nightmare hadn't been able to sway her from her resolve.

Carla had learned from past experience the best way to forget something unpleasant or unbearable was to deliberately turn her thoughts on something pleasant as fast as she could.

To forget Penny and Marc, she made herself think of a life with Cecil Barker, millionaire. No financial burdens. An opportunity to see the world. Access to an unlimited bank account. Paris originals. Finest hotels. Luxury apartments.

Carla sat straight up in bed and threw back the covers. A clear picture of the night Mr. Barker forced her up to his luxury apartment reminded her of something she had seen. In that flash of memory, something clicked in her mind.

She knew, from that moment, it was imperative to encourage Cecil Barker's interest. Her motive, however, could no longer be for personal reasons.

13

Carla looked up from her inventory sheet into the sleepy, blue eyes of Jim Frazer. It was the first time she'd seen him since she'd gotten back from Idaho Springs.

"I'm not a ghost, honey. I'm very much alive and dyin' to hold you in my arms again."

A sudden flush of excitement reminded her she was still the same vulnerable woman she'd always been with him.

"Now, Jim, I told you before—" Her voice cracked.

Flustered and furious at her own inability to control that old melting sensation, she flounced to the cash register, and rang up a "no sale."

Jim covered her hand with his and smiled. "That won't do, baby. I gotta hear it from your own lips." Leaning over the counter, he whispered in her ear, "Meet me at The Hideaway for lunch."

"No, Jim, I can't." Her protest had the hint of a promise.

"See ya." She watched his tall, slim figure saunter through the door.

Her eyes focused on the inventory sheet before her, but her mind was torn between a desire to be in Jim's arms again and a determination to stay away from him.

"Carla, my dear, you look radiant this morning."

Cecil Barker's greeting startled her. He'd never been in her shop before.

"Just came from the real estate office. Someone's interested in purchasing your entire stock of exotic gifts."

Carla stared at him, unable to grasp what he'd said.

"Are you willing to sell your merchandise, piece by piece?" His eyes shifted over the shelves. His attitude was one of urgency. Was this the opportunity she'd been waiting for?

"It all depends on the offer, Mr. Barker." She managed a smile.

"Personally, my first plans were to sell my shop as an established business, plus my house—all in one package deal, if possible."

"Can we discuss it over lunch?"

"I suppose so."

"Can you leave now?"

"It's still my business." She laughed as she slipped her bag over her shoulder, locked the cash register, and stepped from behind the counter.

As she slid into the pretentious Lincoln Continental, she sensed a wave of gratitude that the decision to be with Jim could be postponed.

As they lingered over dessert and coffee at the Holiday Inn, Carla was conscious of an invisible pressure. Mr. Barker seemed nervous as he attempted to convince her that she'd realize a much greater profit by selling each item of her valuable imports separately.

"To be frank with you, my dear, I am the interested buyer. I need your kind of merchandise for my new venture in Central City. Along with my Silverton Inn, I thought it would be quite considerate and profitable to establish a gift shop with items of fine, rare quality for my wealthy patrons."

"And my house? Are you ready to take it off my hands, too?" she bantered.

"We'll discuss that later." The corners of his mouth twisted. This man was not to be underestimated. An attempt to outwit him could prove disastrous. She firmed her lips and lifted her chin. Who was to keep her from trying?

In front of her gift shop, Cecil Barker's eyes skimmed over her. "I'll be in close contact, my dear," he rasped.

Carla smiled and jumped out of the car. Under her breath she said, "You can count on it, big buddy."

Seconds later, Jim stalked through the door. "Why did you keep me waitin' so long?" he scowled. "I called you and they said you were out. No message or anything."

Carla squared her shoulders and kept her voice low. "I told you I don't want to see you anymore, Jim."

"I know you told me that, honey," he whined, "but I can't believe you mean it. Anyway, I thought you'd want to hear my good news." His voice rose.

"Sue's starting the divorce next week. Did you hear me? I'. be free. We can get married, Carla."

Aware of curious glances from browsing customers, Carla whispered, "Jim, please leave. We'll get together, I promise. But only to discuss things privately."

"That's good enough for me, honey. I'll call you tonight."

When Carla got home that evening, Penny had prepared an attractive meal.

"I'm practicing on you, Mom. This is a new dish I found on the back of the calendar. And I made cornmeal muffins from scratch. And look, strawberry shortcake."

"Are you trying to make me fat?" Carla laughed.

The meal was delicious and their communication surprisingly enjoyable. They did the dishes together and laughed a lot.

"Are you staying home this evening?" Carla asked.

"If you want me to. I really shouldn't see Ray so much."

"I'd like to talk awhile. It's been a long time. I haven't had a chance to tell you what happened while I was in Idaho Springs."

Carla's longing for Marc hadn't lessened as the weeks had passed. Just talking to someone about him would bring him closer, she knew.

"You sound mysterious. Was it something terribly exciting?"

"Very. Come on, let's sit down." Carla stuffed a cushion behind her back, stretched her crossed legs out on the couch, and clasped her hands behind her head.

"Maybe you'd better close the front door and lock it, and check the back door, too."

"Is it going to be a scary story?" Penny squealed as she closed doors and locked them. "Now, we're safe." She plopped down at the opposite end of the couch, drew her long legs up under her chin, locked her arms around them and whispered, "Is it a real live mystery?"

"It really is. And what I'm about to say mustn't be repeated to anyone."

"Is it a murder mystery?"

"Everything points that way. But let me start from the beginning. Are you ready?"

"I guess," Penny squeaked.

"It all began on the night of July third at the send-off for Gold Rush Days. We were immediately attracted to each other, Marc Randall and I." Carla felt the blood rise to her forehead.

Penny giggled. "This sounds like a True Romance."

"You might call it Romance and Suspense," Carla smiled. "Please don't interrupt my train of thought."

"All right, I'll be good," Penny promised.

"The next day, Marc took me to Winthrop House up above Central City. It is his aunt's house. His aunt is none other than the much publicized Matilda Winthrop."

"Oh, I've heard of her," said Penny. "Isn't she that wealthy woman that always has her picture in the paper?"

"That's the one," said Carla. "I had already read of her death in the papers, but I soon learned from Marc that there were overtones of mystery about it."

"Does he think it was murder?"

"Let me tell you the clues we've found, and you can draw your own conclusions."

"Is this some kind of game?"

"It's no game, my baby. First, let me tell you about the Kerneys. He's the gardener; she's the housekeeper. They live in an apartment in back of the kitchen. Walt is shifty-eyed and nervous-acting. Sarah is a bird-like woman in appearance, immaculate housekeeper, snoopy, and I believe, malicious. She hates me, I'm sure. Says I'm trying to worm my way into the Winthrop fortune. I don't trust either one of them."

"What made Marc what's-his-name suspicious?"

"Because, he said she was in perfect health as of her last check-up a few days before. The doctor told her she was as young as a woman of fifty."

"Fifty, young?" Penny snickered.

"It's young for seventy. Anyway, that morning Sarah Kerney found her on her bed when she went up with her breakfast. Lying on her back, her head straight on the pillow, not a hair out of place, her arms outside the covers, palms up, and her legs straight down, she was stiff—rigor mortis. Can you picture it?"

"Unnatural, to say the least. In fact, downright creepy."

"That's what Marc said. Yet, the coroner's report was, 'possible natural causes.' Marc is an insurance investigator, and has been working on his aunt's case since her death."

Carla shifted to her side, her head resting on one hand. "Now, let's get back to the clues. Aunt Matilda, I'll call her that, evidently had a gentleman friend. Sarah and Walt both saw him on several occasions, however he always managed to hide his face with a newspaper or napkin or something, so they never got a good look at him. The only description they were able to give was that he was tall, straight and had white hair. They said he was well-mannered and attentive to Aunt Matilda, and they said she seemed more than a little interested in him."

Penny began to giggle again. "Seventy years old? How could anyone that old be interested in anyone?"

"Don't ask me. I'm not seventy," Carla smiled. "Let me get on with the clues. The first was a scrap of paper I found on the kitchen floor. It looked like a column of large sums of money. The first numbers had been torn off, so it was impossible to tell what amount. The interesting part was, on the other side were the initials, 'R. Pow.' It turned out to be Ronald Powell, the man she was interested in. And, after the initials was, 'pd.,' meaning paid, no doubt." She paused for breath, then continued.

"Sarah admitted she had found several papers in the waste basket in the master bedroom. It seems Ronald Powell had spent the night on several different occasions and had used the master bedroom. When Sarah emptied the basket, that scrap had evidently missed the trash compactor." Carla paused again.

"Then, there was a letter Sarah gave to Marc. She admitted taking it from the man's suitcase, with the excuse she was suspicious and wanted to find out more about him."

"What did the letter say?"

"I think I can remember it word for word. Let me think. Oh, yes, it said, 'I am not waiting much longer. If you are not here by Friday, that is it.' There was no name at the top or the bottom. The envelope was addressed to Ronald Powell in care of Miss Matilda Winthrop, and had a Denver postmark."

"Oooh, I'm really getting scared." Penny hugged the pillow.

"There's a lot more," said Carla, leaning forward and pulling her feet under her. "The next day, Marc showed me Aunt Matilda's wardrobe—the most exquisite gowns you can imagine! The loveliest was her wedding dress. It had never been worn. Marc told me the story."

Penny leaned forward eagerly.

"The day before she was to be married, her fiance, while trying to clear a hedge, was thrown from his horse. His neck was broken. She saw it happen from her upstairs window. A terrible tragedy for her. She never married. But, she had scores of admirers all her life."

Carla got up and walked about the room, talking to herself more than to Penny.

"The next afternoon while we were at Winthrop House, I asked Marc if I could try on the wedding gown. I knew it would fit me. I think he wanted me to. You see, he loved his aunt very much. After I put it on, I discovered it had no zipper. I ran downstairs to get Marc to help me. After he fastened all those hooks and eyes . . ."

"This is the romance part, I can tell. When do I get to meet him?"

Carla felt her face getting warm. She sat down again.

"We'll proceed with the clues. When I went back upstairs and began taking the dress off, I noticed the fragrance of violets on the neckline. I called Marc. He came to the same conclusion I did. Someone had worn that dress recently. It had to be Aunt Matilda. But, why? We went through her dresser drawer and found the crystal bottle containing the exquisite French Violette Parfum. Marc said she'd probably gotten it while on one of her many trips abroad."

"She sounds like a storybook character." Penny sighed.

"The next day," Carla continued, "I was left alone while Marc attended to business in Central City. I decided to do a little sleuthing on my own. I knew there must be some family heirlooms somewhere in the house. I started in Aunt Matilda's bedroom."

"And—?"

"In the back of her wardrobe, behind stacks of shoe boxes,

I found the jewel chest. Among the fabulous jewels, but certainly out of place, I found a man's ring. It must have been a lodge ring. A most unique design—downright sinister. Let me draw a sketch of it. Or wait—I remember I drew one for Uncle George just before I left Idaho Springs. I thought he might be able to tell me something about the symbol. I think the slip of paper is still in my blouse pocket. Just a minute, I'll go see."

Carla ran to her room and flipped through hangers in the closet until she found her red and white striped blouse. The piece of paper was still there. Unfolding it, she caught her breath. On the back of her drawing, printed in block letters, were the words, *Ronald Powell.*

Her thoughts went back to the morning she drew the diagram for George. She had plucked the scrap of paper from his shirt pocket, along with his pen. A shiver went through her. She shoved the scrap of paper under her pillow, grabbed a scratch pad from her night table, and hurried back to Penny. Sitting close beside her, her hand shook as she drew the first line on the pad.

"It looked something like this. This is supposed to be a ram's head. It was framed by a hunter's bow. And then there was an arrow piercing through the ears. The tip of the arrow was a large blood-red ruby. The ring itself was brushed yellow gold. The symbol was carved on dark green jade."

Penny put her hands over her eyes. "How gruesome—it's weird, heartless. Whose ring was it? Did Uncle George know what it meant? Where is the ring now?"

"One question at a time, please." Carla put the sketch on the coffee table. "We found out Ronald Powell wore a ring like it. Whether the one I found in the jewel box was his or not, we don't know. Uncle George remembered seeing the symbol somewhere. He couldn't remember where. And, we don't know where the ring is now. The last I heard, it was missing."

"Oh, Mom, I'm worried about you. Are you in danger? Will Marc protect you?"

"If I'm in danger, I doubt if Marc will know about it. You see, we had some differences of opinion. It seems he believes the way you do, so there's a wall between us. I can't possibly meet his standards of morality."

Carla headed for the kitchen. Penny followed close behind her.

"Do you think he's a Christian, Mom?"

"No doubt about it. And I'm a heathen."

Before Carla reached the cupboard, her mind made up to pour a drink for herself, the doorbell rang. They both looked at each other, wide-eyed, then began to laugh.

"I guess we're a little jumpy," said Penny, going to the door. Before opening it, she peeked through the drapes.

"It's Uncle George!" she squealed.

14

Framed in the doorway, George Grant grinned at them. "Didn't you know I was coming? I told Irene to call you."

"That's okay, George. Come on in." Doubts began to form in her mind as Carla thought about the scrap of paper and Ronald Powell's name.

"Irene wanted me to bring the dresses down since they're finished. She's afraid something might happen to them."

"Oh, Uncle George, how sweet of her, and thank you for making that special trip down here just for me."

"Anytime, kid, for you."

"We'll help bring them in," said Carla, running out ahead of them.

The dresses had been wrapped in tissue paper that rustled and crinkled as they were lifted from the back of the station wagon. Holding them high, they were carried to Penny's room, where George stood on a chair and hung them from hooks on the ceiling next to Penny's bridal gown.

"You'll have to make a tunnel through all this froth to get to your bed," George teased.

"She'll manage." Carla pushed him out of the room and down the hall.

"Come on, I'll fix you a sandwich. Are you staying all night?"

She hoped he'd say no. Why was she so uneasy? Surely there was a simple explanation. She'd just ask him about Ronald Powell.

Before they got to the end of the hall, Penny called, "If you'll excuse me, I think I'll get ready for bed. You're still going to give me away, aren't you, Uncle George?"

"You don't think I'd miss an opportunity like that, do you? And believe me, I know plenty to tell." He winked at Carla.

"Oh, you wouldn't," Penny squealed.

"On second thought, maybe I don't know too much about you. Now if it was your mother, that's a different story." He laughed and waved as Carla prodded him down the hall.

As he passed by the coffee table, she saw him swoop up the scrap of paper she had tossed there after showing the drawing to Penny. In the kitchen, she watched him smooth the paper out on the table.

"I see you're still working on your little mystery."

Carla took a deep breath to relieve the tenseness in her chest, then asked, "Did you find out what it means?"

"Pour me some coffee and I'll tell you as much as you should know."

After pouring the coffee, Carla's hand shook as she lifted her cup to her lips, while George appeared even calmer than usual.

"I recognized the symbol the first time you showed it to me, Sis, but I thought the less you knew about it, the better."

"But why? Is it some secret cult or something?"

His eyes were focused on the paper in front of him. "I'd hoped you'd forgotten about it."

"George, don't beat around the bush. Tell me what the symbol means, and while you're at it, what do you know about Ronald Powell?"

Now George was visibly disturbed. "What makes you think I know anything about Ronald Powell?" He crushed the paper in his fist.

"I'll prove it." She swished from the kitchen, flew to her bedroom, snatched the paper from under her pillow, and was back at his side. She spread the creased paper before him.

"I'm sure you recognize this particular piece of paper. I borrowed it from your shirt pocket that morning I left Idaho Springs. I used it to draw this diagram of the ring for you."

Carla peered into George's opaque eyes.

"Tonight, after trying to describe the ring to Penny, I remembered this drawing I'd done for you. It was still in my blouse pocket, but I discovered something I hadn't noticed before."

She flipped the paper over and pointed to the hand-printed letters, *RONALD POWELL*.

After minutes of breathless silence, George raised his eyes from the paper, relaxed against the back of his chair, and grinned at her. "Did you say you were going to fix me a sandwich?"

She knew he was hedging for time. Irritated, she jumped up, pulled the refrigerator door open, then shoved cheese, salami, lettuce and mayonnaise, along with a loaf of dark rye bread, in front of him.

After refilling their cups, she perched on the edge of her chair, elbows on table, chin in hands, and stared at him. George outwardly ignored her, apparently occupied solely with the making of a sandwich. He deliberately spread mayonnaise on a slice of bread, methodically stacked alternate slices of cheese and salami, topped it with lettuce, more mayonnaise and then slapped another slice of bread on top.

Carla was ready to scream when he finally set the sandwich on a napkin, glanced over his shoulder, leaned toward her, and tapped the scrap of paper with his forefinger. She strained to hear his whispered words.

"The Hunters—secret organization—limited membership—my application was accepted—already finished my first assignment—"

The back of her neck seemed to be brushed by a chilling breeze—his assignment, could it be murder?

"What about Ronald Powell—" The words stuck in her throat.

Clutching the sandwich in one hand and the scrap of paper in the other, George leaped to his feet.

"I've talked too much already. I want you to forget everything I've said, do you hear?" He assumed an air of indifference and started for the front door.

"Oh, I almost forgot. Your purse is in the car. Mom said you took hers by mistake. I'll get it."

Carla ran to the closet, grabbed her mother's purse from the top shelf and met George at the door. She trembled as she clutched her own bag to her breast.

"See you tomorrow afternoon. Remember the dress rehearsal and the dinner at Ray's folks. You'll be staying here all night, of course."

"Okay, Sis. And don't forget. Forget!"

She locked the door behind him, scurried to her room, and dumped the contents of her bag on the spread. There it was! Marc's folded handkerchief lay beneath the compact, comb and lipstick. She lifted it by one corner and shook it out. The brushed gold ring set with carved jade seemed to come alive with flashing lights captured by the blood-red ruby.

Reluctant to touch the ring that had suddenly become a symbol of evil, she knew it must be put in a safe place, perhaps later to be used as evidence against its owner. Its former hiding place, in Aunt Matilda's wardrobe, gave her an idea. She shuddered as she picked it up and dropped it in the bottom shoe box in her own closet.

Driven by a feeling of contamination, she washed her hands with soap, and once again by her bed, she gazed dreamily at Marc's handkerchief. Almost reverently, she pressed it to her cheek and fell across the bed as sobs revealed her deep longing.

"Oh, Marc darling, I need you."

Heedless of consequences, she reached for the phone and dialed Irene's number.

"Irene, don't be alarmed. Nothing's wrong—yes, George left a little while ago—the dresses are beautiful, but that's not the reason I called. Do you have Marc's number? . . . California? Why? His mother had a stroke? Irene—did he leave a number to call? Wait, I'll write it down—"

She could hardly wait for Irene to hang up. She dialed the long distance number and marveled at the swiftness of the connection. At the sound of his deep, beloved voice, her mouth was so dry, she had to swallow several times before she said, "Marc—is that you? I heard about your mother. Is she all right? Oh, yes, I'm fine—something came up I thought you should know. The ring—I found it in my bag. It's been at my mother's. I took hers by mistake. George brought it to me tonight. Marc, I'm afraid he's mixed up in this somehow. He told me the symbol on the ring is used by an organization he belongs to—"

What was Marc saying? Her ears roared. Her mind felt numb. She held her breath and listened.

"You will? Day after tomorrow, yes. Do you think your mother will be well enough for you to leave her? I do want to see you—"

After she hung up, she could hardly believe the conversation had taken place. It must have been a dream—a most wonderful dream.

Running down the hall, she called Penny's name. "Wake up, wake up. He's coming here. Marc's coming to your wedding. It's really true."

Penny sat up, rubbing her eyes. "What made him decide? Are your differences settled?"

"No, but he's coming to see me. That's enough for now."

Carla pulled Penny out of bed and guided her back to her room. "Come on, wake up and share my happiness with me. I want to talk."

Carla felt like a teenager again, talking to her best girl friend about the secrets of her heart.

"His voice was the same as I remembered it. Deep and resonant, masculine—you know. There was so much concern in it and I think, love, too. I didn't realize how much I missed him 'til I heard his voice." Tears blurred her vision. She put her hands over her face and moaned.

"Oh, Penny, what can I do? I'm tired of walls and guilt. How can I be like you and Marc?"

Penny threw her arms around her and held her close.

"Oh, my little Mom. Do you really want to know? Just a minute—let me get my Bible—are you sure you want to know?"

Carla closed her eyes, her hands clasped in her lap, and waited for Penny. In her heart, she whispered, "God, I want to do what You want me to."

Penny knelt beside the bed, her Bible open. "Mom, I'll read a few verses and you listen to the words like God is saying them. Will you?"

Carla nodded.

"'For God so loved the world that he gave his only begotten Son, that whosoever believeth in him should not perish but have everlasting life.' 'All have sinned and come short of the glory of God.' 'The wages of sin is death, but the gift of God is life through Jesus Christ our Lord.' 'But as many as received him, to them gave he power to become the sons of God, even to them that believe on his name.'"

Penny stopped reading. The room had suddenly become a holy place. The words Carla had heard were living words. Was this what Marc meant when he told her to listen with her heart? She

113

knew God was speaking to her.

Penny's bowed head and clasped hands on the open Bible brought such a sense of conviction and unworthiness to her conscience, she slipped to her knees beside Penny.

"Tell me what to say to Him," she whispered.

Her eyes still closed, Penny said, "Just tell Him you know you're a sinner, and that Jesus died for your sins and rose again. Tell Him you believe that, and you want Him to come into your life and save your soul."

Carla trembled with excitement. To be forgiven for all her sins! Could this be true? She had to know.

"Dear God," she stammered, "I'm glad You died for me and forgave all my sins. I don't know why You did. I'm not worth it, but thank You, anyway, Lord Jesus. I do believe. Please come into my heart and save my soul."

"Mom, you're saved." Penny's eyes glistened with tears. "You belong to God's family now!"

"Yes, I know." Carla sensed an awesome assurance unknown to her before. "He was here, in this room. He took a load off my heart. Penny, the wall is down! I'm free!"

She hugged Penny. "I love you. I love Jesus. Wasn't that a wonderful thing for Him to do for me?"

The next morning, awakened by the telephone, Carla Preston's first thought was "Jesus." She was surprised at how easy it was to whisper His name. Her whole being seemed to be filled with an overwhelming love for Him.

She answered the persistent ringing. "*Rich?* Where are you? No, no—come on out—don't stay at a hotel—plenty of room— yes. Hurry, now—I'll have breakfast ready for you. 'Bye, now."

"It was your grandfather," Carla answered Penny's questioning look. "They'll be here for breakfast. Get dressed as quick as you can. I'll need some help."

Carla wondered at her peace of mind and enthusiasm, even for unexpected company for breakfast. There was no frustration or irritation. She wanted to sing, but the only song she knew that would express her feelings was, "Oh, What a Beautiful Morning,

Oh, What a Beautiful Day." Penny smiled at her and nodded her head knowingly.

At the sound of closing car doors, Carla walked out on the porch to greet them. Penny was beside her.

"Welcome! You timed it just right."

Gladys, Rich Preston's second wife, lumbered up the steps. Carla kissed her on the cheek. Rich bounded up behind her, took Carla in his arms and kissed her mouth. She shrugged off her momentary mental cringe.

Inside, Gladys dropped her huge bag on a chair and proceeded straight to the kitchen.

"Coffee smells good." Carla had forgotten how loud Gladys was.

Rich Preston's eyes swept over Penny as he held her at arm's length.

"Let me look at my little granddaughter. What a beautiful young lady you turned out to be!"

"You're still as handsome as I remembered you, Granddad."

"When do we eat? I'm starved." Gladys interrupted.

Subconsciously, Carla wondered what attraction this crude woman held for a man like Richard Preston.

At the table, she avoided the sight of Gladys' ravenous appetite, and focused her attention on Rich. His expensive tailored suit, plus an oversized diamond flashing from a little finger ring, increased her curiosity about his source of income.

Suddenly, Carla's body stiffened, her throat burned, her eyes blurred. That ring on his right hand! Penny must have noticed it at the same time.

"Where did you get that ring, Granddad? It's just like the one Mom—" Her voice faded away at Carla's warning glance.

During the interval of awkward silence, Rich Preston's blue eyes iced up. "What about a ring just like this?" His voice was brittle.

Under his piercing gaze, calmness seemed to wrap itself about Carla. "I don't know much, Rich. My sister's husband belongs to an organization that uses a symbol like that."

"Where does he live? What's his name?"

"He lives in Idaho Springs. His name is George Grant."

"You musta seen him when you was up there in June," Gladys broke in.

"Shut up!" Rich Preston's face seemed to turn a purplish hue. He shoved his chair back and stalked out the front door. As they all sat staring at each other, they heard the car start and tires squeal as he drove away.

"Don't pay any attention to him." Gladys put another slice of bread in the toaster. "If you ask me, they're all a bunch of boys playing at cops and robbers with all their mysterious meetings and secret signs.

Gladys got up and paced the floor. "I don't see why he had to take my luggage with him. You got a drink in the house, Carla?"

Carla automatically reached under the sink and brought out a bottle of whiskey. After pouring some in a glass, she was suddenly struck with a sense of guilt. What would Jesus think of her? She poured the rest of the contents down the sink. Gladys looked comical with her eyes and mouth wide open.

"What did you do that for? Are you nuts?"

"No, she's not nuts." Penny stepped between them. "She's a Christian."

Gladys stared at them for a long time, then slumped into her chair, dropped her head on her arms and groaned.

When she raised her head she said, "You'd never believe this, Penny, but I'm a Christian, too. When I was a little girl, I asked Jesus to come into my heart." She began to sob.

"I don't know how I got so far away from Him."

15

Gladys raised her head from her arms, pulled a tissue from the neck of her blouse, and blew her nose.

"What should I do, Carla? What would you do?"

Carla put her arm on her shoulder. "Would you like to talk about it first?"

"Yeah, I'd like to tell you a few things, but I don't think Penny ought to hear."

"I understand. I've got a lot to do anyway." Penny left the room.

"Are you sure you want to hear?" Gladys blew her nose again. Carla poured two cups of coffee and sat opposite her, chin in hands. Gladys reached over and patted Carla's head. "I'm so glad you're a Christian, Carla. I really want to come back to the Lord, too."

Carla smiled at her. "I know you do. I'm sure it will help if you talk about how you got away in the first place."

"I shouldn't have married him. I knew he wasn't the right sort. In some crooked deal from the time I met him—always some woman. He's good-lookin'. Women fall for him—especially old women. He has a way with them."

Blood drained from Carla's heart. Could it be? Richard Preston—Ronald Powell? Even the initials were the same.

"You okay, girl?"

Carla nodded. "Gladys, you mentioned a trip he took in June. Where did he go?"

"Oh, I went with him on that one. That lodge, or whatever he belongs to, takes him all over. I learned a long time ago not to ask any questions. The reason I remember that trip was because he stayed away so long. He left me in Denver at the Brown Palace." She smiled. "It was comfortable enough."

"Do you know where he went, Gladys?" Carla was impatient.

"Somewhere in the mountains. That's one reason he gave for not taking me. He knows I hate mountain driving. I think it was Central City. He hired a car—had to be a Cadillac, you know."

Carla recalled the letter Sarah had gotten from Ronald Powell's suitcase. "Why did he use the name Ronald Powell?" She shot the question at Gladys, and watched her bite her lip.

"He didn't want you or Penny to ever find out. You see, he had his name changed after he was released from prison."

"What was the crime?" Carla held her breath, sure of Gladys' answer.

"Fraud, or if you prefer, 'the old confidence game!'"

"That must have been awful for you, Gladys."

"I was well provided for. You see, I was shrewd enough to demand my share of every take." Gladys looked down at her clasped hands. "I'm sure, now, that was wrong in God's sight. Do you think I should give it all back to him?"

"I don't know what to say. I'm sure God will let you know. I'll pray for you." A sense of awesome power came over her. She had a Heavenly Father she could talk to!

"I know what I should do, Carla. I should leave him right now and never see him again. You and Penny have brought me to my senses. I'll go to my sister's in Greeley." Her faced glowed.

"If you're sure that's what you want to do, I'll take you to the bus stop. What should I tell Rich when he comes back?"

"Just tell him I left. You don't have to say where. Just tell him I don't want him to know."

They wasted no time, but went directly to the depot, where perfect connections were made. Gladys was soon on her way to her sister's home.

On her way back, a sense of guilt overshadowed Carla. She thought of her deceit with Mr. Barker the day before. How far was she willing to go to get her house sold?

Before she realized what she was doing, she pulled into a parking space in front of the real estate office. She breezed up to the counter.

"I've decided not to sell my house or my business. Please take them off your sales list."

The burden was lifted. The guilt was gone. God had restored her self-respect. She didn't have to leave this small town after all.

Light hearted and light-stepped, she shopped at the market before heading for home. A glance in the rearview mirror reflected a green compact car definitely tailgating. Before she could pick up speed, it swerved out from behind her, and came up close beside her, forcing her to the curb. Suddenly it swung in front of her, brakes screaming. Two men jerked her door open and pulled her out.

She was being abducted—in broad daylight—by Mr. Barker's bodyguards! Why wasn't she afraid? Acutely aware of her Protector, she relaxed in the back seat of the green compact car. When they drove into a narrow country lane, past a grove of trees, she knew this must be Cecil Barker's ranch house.

Ushered into the big man's presence with a flourish, as if they were trying to say, no problem, the two men left her alone with Mr. Cecil Barker.

Carla, calm but indignant, lifted her chin.

"This is quite an unexpected invitation, dear Mr. Barker."

"We'll dispense with the preliminaries, my dear." He sounded ominous. "Why did you take your property off the market? You knew I was interested."

Ignoring his question, Carla looked about the room. She unconsciously observed the massive furniture, designed for the massive man. The somber colors, the dim lighting, the smell of sweet pipe tobacco—an involuntary wave of nausea swept over her.

She strolled to the picture window. No sign of life as far as she could see. She faced his penetrating stare.

"Mr. Barker, I don't appreciate your underhanded methods. This is your second act of abduction. If you'll call your men, I'd like to get to my parked car. As for giving my reasons for taking my property off the market, that's *my* business."

Cecil Barker shifted his bulk in his mammoth chair. "You are most unpredictable, my dear. The last time I saw you, you led me to believe you had changed your mind about my proposal of marriage. Why did you do that?"

"I must confess I had ulterior motives at that time. Something has changed my mind. My future is in Someone else's hands now. I'm unable to explain it, so don't ask me."

"Is it Marc Randall?" He sneered his distaste.

"Mr. Barker, I've wasted enough time here. I want to get back home. This is a busy day for me."

He struggled to his feet. "That's right. Your daughter's getting married tomorrow night." He tapped a small bell on his desk, and before the men appeared, his parting remark was, "Forgive the interruption in your busy schedule."

Neither bodyguard spoke on the way back to her car, and even when she got out, their eyes were fixed on the road ahead.

Carla began to tremble when she stopped in her own driveway. Was it fear or relief? She tried to review the events of the morning. There was Rich Preston's outburst and sudden departure, the overwhelming revelation of his name change to Ronald Powell, his conviction on fraud charges and the subsequent prison term. Then, the startling fact of Gladys being a Christian, and their amazing bond of friendship because of it. Her unexpected decision to keep her house and business was climaxed only by her abduction. Fear or relief, whatever—it was enough to make anyone tremble.

As she got out of the car, she looked at her house with new interest. Somehow, it had taken on an air of respectability.

Penny met her at the door. "Mom, what took you so long?"

Carla took one look and began to laugh.

"Here comes the bride," Carla sang out.

Penny slow-stepped across the room. "Do you notice anything?"

"The bridal veil sets off the jeans and sneakers beautifully! What is that lovely fragrance?"

"You did notice. Look, real orange blossoms from California! Can you guess who from?"

"Marc? Did he really? Let me smell. How beautiful they look on you. A crown of real orange blossoms."

"Read the card."

Carla read out loud, "To a lovely girl I've never met. May Christ be the head of your house." It was signed, Marc Randall.

Penny lifted the wreath from her head and put it back in the florist box. "I'll keep it in the refrigerator—come with me, I want to show you something."

She opened the door of the refrigerator. "This box has your name on it."

Carla squealed, "For me?" She pressed it to her breast and

closed her eyes. "How thoughtful of him," she said and lifted the lid. Penny stared over her shoulder.

"Violets! How romantic! What does the card say?"

Tears blurred Carla's vision of the nosegay of royal-blue violets nestled in shredded, waxed paper. Their fragrance reminded her of the perfume on Aunt Matilda's wedding gown; their fresh beauty was a symbol of romance.

She took the small card from the box. "The color of your eyes." That's all it said, but it told her he remembered her eyes, and that the violets were an expression of his unspoken words.

"Mom, is he really that romantic? I can hardly wait to see him!"

"Me either," Carla kissed Penny's cheek, put the box back in the refrigerator, and ran to the car. She'd forgotten her groceries were still there.

Should she tell Penny about the horrible experience she'd had? She didn't want to worry her. But she'd like to tell her how the Lord took care of her, and how she wasn't afraid. Some other time.

Just as they finished a light lunch, Rich Preston called. Carla answered, "No, Rich, she isn't here—I'm sorry I can't tell you— I'd rather you wouldn't." There was a moment of panic, then peace.

To Penny, she said, "Your grandfather is coming back here. Gladys doesn't want him to know where she is. How do I keep it from him without lying?"

"You can just say Gladys doesn't want you to tell."

"That's what I'll say."

"Mom, I promised Ray's mother I'd be there right after lunch to help with the dinner for the family this evening. Mind if I use your car?"

"Go ahead." She thought at once of meeting Rich Preston alone, and again turned her fears over to the Lord.

After Penny left, Carla decided to try on her dress. She wanted to see how the violets looked with it. In her room, she slipped into the filmy, sky-blue billows of chiffon, zipped up the back and lifted the clustered violets from their box.

As she held them at the softly draped neckline, she felt his presence before she saw him leaning in the doorway. Rich Preston's open admiration was embarrassing.

"You shouldn't have left your front door open." He stepped into her room. "I didn't realize you were such an attractive woman, Carla. Herb was a lucky man."

Carla placed the violets back in the box. "If you'll excuse me, I'll change and be right with you, Rich. Pour yourself a cup of coffee." Would he be dismissed that easily? She asked the Lord to be with her.

He left without a word. She changed as quickly as she could and took her treasured gift from Marc back to the kitchen. Rich was at the table, a cup of coffee in front of him. He jumped to his feet, pulled her chair out and poured a cup of coffee for her.

Carla watched his display of charming attention and understood Lucy Lovelace a little better. And Aunt Matilda? Was she in love with him? Could he have killed her?

"You look distressed, my dear." His manner changed from concern to cold indifference. "I had to come back, you know. There are too many loose ends here. First, where is Gladys?"

"She told me not to tell you."

"And do you think you can keep it from me?" His hand shot out and grabbed hers in a grasp that made her fingers tingle. She held her breath, conscious of the hard light in his eyes. He dropped her hand on the table.

"I'm sorry if I hurt you. I have to know where she is. I can't explain anything to you, but I'm asking you to trust me."

He touched the strange ring on his right hand. "You know something about this, don't you? Did you discuss it with Gladys?"

Carla was aware of his desperation. "She seemed to think it was a lodge ring—said you were a member of a group of men that acted like children with all your mysteries and secrets."

"Did she mention the trip in June?"

"Yes, she said you were gone a long time—she thought in Central City. She stayed at the Brown Palace in Denver."

His eyes seemed to bore through her. "What do you know about me?"

"She told me you had your name changed to Ronald Powell." She waited for his reaction.

"Rich, do you know Ronald Powell is a suspect in the death of Matilda Winthrop?"

16

Carla Preston was glad Rich didn't stay long after her bombshell. The mental stress of the morning and the tense scene with Rich were almost too much.

She welcomed the physical activities of the rest of the day: the arrival of her family; the game of going through the tunnel of bridesmaids' dresses to get a look at wedding gifts spread out on Penny's bed; George's restless visits to the kitchen for drinks, using his own whiskey; the ardent conversations with her mother and Irene about Jesus, her new-found love; dinner with Ray's family. And after that, the wedding rehearsal.

When they got back home, Irene followed Carla into her room. "Wasn't that a beautiful rehearsal? The ceremony, the message, everything—how important that both the bride and groom are Christians!"

"I'm beginning to see that, Irene. I think I know why Marc never told me he loved me. He knew he couldn't marry an unbeliever."

"Aren't you glad he didn't? If he'd been weak enough to let you think you were okay, you may never have found the Lord." Irene sat beside Carla on the bed.

"Why was I so blind?" Carla clasped her hands under her chin. "I'm so glad I know Him now."

George stood in the doorway, unobserved. "I can see this whole family has gone fanatic. Where does that leave me? All alone, by myself? In that case I'll go find me a drinking partner." He stalked out.

"Don't worry about him, Sis. His bark is worse than his bite." Irene smiled wistfully. "I've been praying he'd see his need for Jesus."

"Irene, did you pray for me?"

"I sure did—and He answered."

"I wish I knew how to pray. My prayers sound ignorant and childish."

"That's the way the Lord likes them, childlike. But I think it takes practice, too. And I learned if you pray out loud it keeps your mind from wandering. You pay more attention to what you're saying and Who you're talking to."

"I'd like to get a Bible of my own. I've got this one Penny loaned me, but . . ."

Irene jumped up. "I almost forgot. I bought you one—just like mine—a lot of footnotes so you can understand it better." She was gone and back in less than a minute.

"My very own Bible!" Carla held it reverently. On the first page, Irene had written, "To my wonderful Sis. Don't just go through the Bible; let the Bible go through you. I love you, Irene."

As soon as she could, Carla got ready for bed, propped the pillows behind her head, and opened her Bible to the Book of Genesis.

She'd always thought the Bible was a closed book. She'd never been able to understand it before. But as she read the creation account, the power of God filled her with awesome reverence.

She put the Bible on her night stand, slipped out of bed to her knees, and was acutely aware that her spirit was in direct contact with her Heavenly Father.

Wrapped in His love, all earthly thoughts gave way to heavenly sleep.

The familiar ripple of filmy curtains and filtered sunbeams across her bed heralded the morning. Penny's wedding day!

Carla leaped out of bed, fell on her knees and thanked the Lord for such a good night's rest and for the beautiful day, jumped in and out of the shower and breezed into the kitchen where her mother was busy with breakfast.

"Mother, you didn't have to do that! I planned to cook for *you* this morning."

"I was too excited to sleep late. Do you think the others will want to eat with us?"

"I do," said Penny, shuffling in. She wore a faded terry cloth robe, her hair in huge curlers.

"If Ray could see you now," Carla laughed.

Penny covered her face with her hands. "I'd die," she said. Then dramatically she moaned, "I can't see him all day! He isn't supposed to see me until I come down the aisle in my wedding gown—veil over my face." She hummed the wedding march, circled the kitchen in slow steps and strolled out the door.

"You character," Carla laughed.

"What's so funny?" Irene came through the door, kissed her mother and flopped in a chair. "Well, this is the big day. I'm starting out tired."

"When did George get in?" asked Carla.

"I don't know. Couldn't get to sleep 'til after two. How did he get in? Does he have a key to your house?"

"I don't remember giving him one. He could have taken the extra from the nail in the laundry room. I'll ask him for it when he gets up."

The telephone was in constant use all morning and afternoon. Ray called at least five times. Each bridesmaid had questions about this or that. One time it was for Carla. It was Jim, insistent and impatient, demanding an answer. Then *the call* came through at two-thirty sharp.

"Marc, I've been waiting to hear from you—around four-thirty? Of course, I want you to come right out. Do you want me to meet you at the airport? Maybe you're right. I should stick around here. I'll be looking for that yellow cab! 'Bye, now."

She knew her excitement showed when she turned from the wall phone. "That was Marc."

"No-o-o-o," they all said in unison.

Carla's neck felt hot; then the warmth crept up to her face and into the roots of her hair.

"Mom, you're blushing," Penny teased.

Carla ran to her room and closed her door. She had to be alone to think about what Marc had said. It wasn't much to go on—but she'd see him in two hours. That was enough. Irene tapped her door.

"Do you want to be alone?"

"No, of course not. I just felt silly standing there, red-faced before everyone. I'm glad you're here. Sit down. I want to ask you something."

"You love him, don't you?" Irene sat beside her on the bed.

"You know I do. I was never able to hide it, even from Marc. But give me some advice. Should I tell him right off that I know Jesus now, or should I wait awhile?"

"I see what you mean. You're afraid if you tell him right away, he may think you're trying to force him into something. Right?"

"Something like that. But on the other hand, I know he'll never commit himself to me as long as he thinks I'm an unbeliever. Do you think he might be able to tell I've changed?"

"Why don't you let the Lord lead you? He'll show you what to do."

"Are you sure?" Then Carla laughed. "Of course He will."

It was hard to keep away from the front window, and when Carla saw the yellow cab, she ran out to meet Marc. He took her arm, bent over her and whispered, "How's my Little Peanut?"

She introduced him to Penny, and while greetings were exchanged with the rest of the family, Carla said, "Make yourself comfortable, Marc. I'll get some cold drinks for us."

George followed her out to the kitchen and whispered, "Let me add a little flavor to mine." He brought a flask from his hip pocket. "You really like the guy, don't you, Sis—and don't give me that Mona Lisa smile."

He hovered over her while she poured Pepsi Cola over ice. "How much does he know about what I told you the other night?"

"He's investigating Matilda Winthrop's death." Carla bit her lip. Maybe George shouldn't know so much.

"How does he think she died?" George ran his hand through his hair and gulped his drink.

"We aren't sure yet." Carla brushed past him with the tray of drinks.

Penny swept over to Carla and whispered in her ear. "Oh, Mom, he's just like you said."

Carla glanced at Marc. There was that same twinkle of amusement that had quickened her heart the first night she saw him.

She had to be alone with him. She had to know if he really loved her. At the first conversation lull, she jumped up, ran to her room, grabbed her shoulder bag, and whisked to the front door.

"Mother, do you think you and Irene can keep Penny calm for an hour or so! Marc has to check in at the hotel." She gave her car keys to Marc. "Do you think you can drive my Japanese beer can? That's what George calls it."

Marc looked out of place in her little compact. She snuggled up to him; he put his arm about her shoulder.

"One nice thing about it—close quarters," he said. She looked up to see the crinkled smile she knew would be there. "Is there a park we could stroll in—get some fresh air—feed the ducks, or something?"

"Washington Park isn't far. Take a right at the next through street. And, before I forget, I want to thank you for Penny's lovely gift. She never dreamed she'd have real orange blossoms for her wedding." She hugged his arm. "And violets for me . . ."

"Did you like them?"

He circled the park and after selecting a shady spot, leaped out, tucked her hand under his arm, and strolled down the narrow path. The familiar gesture took her breath away.

"Marc, I've missed you so much." She was aware of his guarded silence. Dear God, what should she do?

They took the path around the duck pond and sat on a bench close by. Marc's attention seemed riveted on the ducks. He picked up bits of bread left by picnickers, tossed them into the pond and watched the ducks dive under, their tails and feet sticking straight up.

After a while he leaned back, put his arm around her shoulders, stretched his legs out, and took a deep breath.

"I've missed you too, Little Peanut. More than I thought possible. Since your call the other night I haven't been able to think of anything else . . ."

Carla put her fingers on his lips. "Before you say any more, I have something to tell you. First, I want to apologize for the awful way I talked to you the last time we were together. My only explanation is, 'There's no wrath like that of a woman scorned.'"

She buried her face in her hands. "I'm so ashamed of the way I threw myself at you time after time. And every time you held me off. You see, I didn't understand you had to, because I was an unbeliever—but now . . ."

"Carla, what are you trying to say?" He held her face in his hands and looked deep into her eyes. "Can it be . . ."

"Yes, Marc, yes. Jesus is my Saviour, too. Now, I understand."

"It's true," he whispered. "No more walls."

In the deep shadows of the leafy park his kiss, soft and tender, was like a benediction.

"Beautiful Carla, I love you." His first words of love filled her with awe that left no room for triumph.

He pulled her to her feet and held her close. After a few minutes, he held her at arm's length. His eyes twinkled with amusement. "First mission accomplished," he said.

"Now, back to Penny. It's her big day. After the wedding, we'll take up where we left off."

Carla threw her arms around his neck. "Oh, my darling, I love you, too."

The rest of the day, the fact that Marc loved her and had said so never left her thoughts. Outwardly, she entered into the activities surrounding her, but her heart sang over and over, he loves me.

Her singing heart continued until they were all seated in their places in church, and the first chords of the wedding march sounded.

At that moment, her full attention rested on Penny. As she watched her lovely daughter come down the aisle on George's arm, cheeks flushed, eyes sparkling, lips parted in a half-smile, tears of joy washed Carla's eyes.

Silently, Carla thanked God for Penny, pure and innocent, her whole life before her—and for Ray, a fine Christian man, dedicated to serving the Lord all his life.

It seemed like hours later that Carla was alone with Marc, at last. He drove back to Washington Park and found a space overlooking the lake. Without a word, he removed the nosegay of violets, placed them on the dashboard, and folded her in his arms. Rapturous moments passed in silence, lips pressed together. Then, moments of continued silence, their heads resting against the back of the seat.

Marc lifted her hand to his lips and kissed the tips of her fingers. "I love you, my Little Peanut."

She turned her head toward him. "Why?" she asked. He chuckled.

"Does there have to be a reason for love? I knew it when I saw Lillian Russell rustle through the lobby that night. Trumpets blared in my heart—there she is!"

"But you took so long to say so."

"I wanted to shout it out again and again, and I wanted to whisper it in your ear. Something stopped me every time." He kissed her fingers again. "I'm sorry I hurt you."

"My silly pride was hurt, that's all. I guess you'd better take me home. Mother and Irene plan to go back tonight. They don't want to miss church in the morning. I'd like to see them before they leave."

"Let me tell you my plans. If it's all right with you, I'll keep your car tonight and come by for you early in the morning. We'll have breakfast at the airport."

"Do you have to leave so soon?"

"Yes, but I plan to come right back if my mother shows any signs of improvement. I'm getting a private nurse to stay with her at home. She's much happier in her own house." He paused a moment.

"I think she's been trying to tell me something. Her eyes look almost desperate. I'm sure it has something to do with Ronald Powell, because when I showed her the name, her eyes flew open wide, and she tried to mumble something. It's really pathetic to see her that way."

"Oh, Marc, my darling, I'm so sorry. Can't you bring her back with you? Maybe she could stay at Winthrop House."

"She'd never agree. Very independent woman. She loves California and won't leave."

When they were almost home, Carla said, "Marc, what should I do with that horrible ring?"

"I'll take it, Little Peanut. Is it at your house?"

Carla nodded. "Do you want to know where I hid it? In the back of my closet in the bottom shoe box." She laughed. "What's good enough for Aunt Matilda is good enough for me."

There were no cars in the driveway when they got to Carla's house.

"You don't suppose they left without saying Good-bye?"

"Maybe they aren't back from the wedding. I'll go in with you to check and pick up the ring."

There was a note from her mother on the coffee table. "Honey, I'm sorry we had to leave without seeing you, but we want to get back before it starts to rain. Let us hear from you soon. We all love you. Mother."

Carla gave the note to Marc and went for the ring. As she placed it in his hand, a sense of loneliness came over her. A premonition of danger crossed her mind. She dismissed the thought. It could be natural to feel apprehensive, since this was the first time she'd ever been alone in her house at night.

"You're not afraid are you, Little Peanut?"

She lifted her lips to his and clung to him. Reluctant to let him go, she said, "I know Someone is with me, Marc. But if I could only see Him or touch Him, it would help a lot."

She tried to act brave as she let him out and locked the door behind him. The distant rumble of thunder didn't help.

17

Carla Preston leaned against the door and shivered as the storm rumbled closer. As she got ready for bed, she had to remind herself she wasn't alone. Wrapped in the shiny blue robe and all the courage she had, she decided to make one last check through the house.

Shallow-breathed and on tiptoe, she switched on lights and tried all the doors. The fury of the storm increased until the house was spotlighted with jagged lightning and shaken under the constant roll of thunder.

"Oh, Lord," she whispered, "forgive me for being afraid. I know You're here with me, but I'm still afraid."

Outside Penny's door, Carla listened. She could pretend Penny was there. But why try to fool herself? With an added spurt of courage, she stepped in and turned on the light.

She gazed at the orderly, lifeless room and felt its silence. She switched off the light, closed the door and reeled back to her room, stabbed with loneliness.

On her knees, throat dry, chest tight, she asked the Lord for protection while the rain slashed her window.

Beneath the covers, her head buried in the pillow, loud knocking could be heard above the storm. She sat up and listened. There it was again. Louder and more persistent this time. Frozen with fear, she waited. Then someone called her name. It came from her bedroom window.

Shocked into action, she leaped out of bed and peeked out. Another flash of lightning revealed the drenched figure of a man—hair, glistening silver.

"Rich! What are you doing here?" she screamed.

"Let me in. They're after me. Hurry!"

Carla grabbed her robe, flew to the front door, and before she could open it more than a crack, Rich squeezed in.

"Don't turn on the lights. I don't think they saw where I came. They'll be searching the neighborhood."

"Oh, Rich, what kind of trouble are you in?"

"Do you have anything I can change into? I'm soaked."

"Come in the kitchen. Don't drip all over the carpet. I'll turn the oven on. That's the best I can do."

"Just don't turn the lights on," he warned again.

Carla fumbled in the dark for the kettle and instant coffee. The peak of the storm seemed to be over. She was amazed at her calmness in the face of real danger. Intermittent flashes of lightning showed her where Rich was. Was he telling the truth?

"Do you want to talk, Rich?"

"I hate to upset you this way, Carla. I guess I'd better explain. The only drawback—it might put you in danger."

Carla felt the blood leave her head. What was that verse Irene had showed her? "God hath not given us the spirit of fear . . ."

After hesitating a minute, Rich said, "You see, they think I have the deed to Winthrop Estate. I don't have it. She was ready to give it to me that night . . ."

In a flash of lightning, Carla saw Rich rest his head in his hands. She heard his breath catch in his throat.

"How did she die?" She knew the question was brutal, but she had to know.

"It was to be an evening to remember," he groaned. "It certainly turned out that way. Matilda Winthrop was an unusual woman. She made me feel worthy and important. I'm sure she would have married me if I'd been free to ask her. I couldn't tell her I was married—didn't want to hurt her—knew about the tragedy of her first love."

Carla felt him brush by her. She recalled the times at Winthrop House when she was surrounded by things Matilda loved, the kindred spirit she felt with her. For a moment she imagined herself as Matilda Winthrop in the presence of the man she loved.

She heard him pull his chair up to the table and knew he leaned toward her when his breath touched her cheek with his next words.

"I'd never seen her so lovely, and happy, too. I know she was happy. She wore a white dress and smelled of violets. In the candlelight there wasn't a wrinkle on her face. We ate, drank, and danced all evening. I hated myself for what I had to do . . ."

Carla held her breath.

"The Chief Hunter does all the planning. I was assigned to Matilda Winthrop while she was visiting her sister in Beverly Hills, since that is my area. The organization managed an invitation to a farewell party given by Mrs. Randall for her sister, Matilda Winthrop.

"At first, I played the old game—promised to visit her in Central City while I was there on business." Bitterly, he said, "I didn't tell her *she* was my business."

Just then Carla heard a car coming down her street. She jumped up, colliding with Rich as both lunged through the dining room door to the front window. Headlights could be seen about halfway down the block. Motionless, they watched it cruise by her house, slowing to a stop two doors down.

"It's them," Rich said, under his breath. "I wonder if they know of our connection?"

They watched the car move on until it came to the intersection. Under the street light, the dark green compact was a familiar sight to Carla. A gasp escaped her lips.

She had to get away from Rich! Carla ran to her room and closed the door as panic began to mount. She searched the nightstand for the little flashlight pencil and dialed Marc's hotel room. Her lungs ached from holding her breath before he finally answered.

Unable to make a sound, she tried over and over to force words out, but only a wheeze was audible. She heard him repeat, "Carla, is that you? Is something wrong?"

Her door opened. Rich was in her room. She heard Marc say, "I'll be right over," just before she felt Rich's rough hand over her mouth, and a jolt on the back of her neck.

Carla didn't know how long she'd been unconscious. Her head ached. She was in her bed. Her light was on. Dazed, she recognized Marc as he bent over her. He bathed her forehead and crooned, "My Little Peanut, my Little Peanut. Please be all right."

She was still unable to make a sound. She could tell he knew she was conscious. He lifted her up and propped pillows behind her. "As soon as you can, tell me what happened and I'll call the police. Who was it? Do you know?"

"Rich Preston," she wheezed. "I let him in. Someone was after him."

"That's enough. Rest now."

She closed her eyes and tried to remember some of the things Rich had said. Marc should know. Her head ached. Her thoughts were muddled. The next thing she knew, two policemen were in the room. Marc lifted her head from the pillow.

"Wake up, Little Peanut. Are you able to answer some questions now?"

"How could I have gone to sleep?"

"Reaction from the blow, no doubt," said one of the men. "Now, if you are able, we'd like a description of this man, Rich Preston.

Carla's throat was relaxed. It was good to make sounds again. "Rich Preston is also Ronald Powell. He had his name legally changed. He is my father-in-law. My husband is dead. I'm afraid Rich is in serious trouble."

Marc stepped between Carla and the men. "I don't think it's necessary to question her any further now. I'll give you a detailed description of Ronald Powell. You see, he's the prime suspect in my aunt's death. There's been an APB on him since our latest evidence against him."

Carla heard Marc's description of Rich Preston/Ronald Powell. "His most outstanding feature is thick, white hair. A little over sixty, ruddy complexion, bright blue eyes, stands straight— almost six feet."

"Thank you, Mr. Randall, and you, too, Mrs. Preston. We'll let you know when he's in custody."

Carla shivered. That poor man! Should she tell them about the Hunters? Those men in the dark green compact were hunting for Rich. What was Mr. Barker's role in this?

Marc called from the living room. "I'm staying right here, Little Peanut. Try to get some sleep."

She lay back on the pillows. Her head still hurt. What had he hit her with? Probably his fist. He must have panicked. He wasn't a violent man. She'd seen his tender side. He couldn't have murdered Matilda Winthrop—but, how could he prove it?

Carla got up and made it to the living room. She sat on a hassock close to Marc's knees. He rubbed the back of her neck and shoulders. "I'm glad you're feeling better."

"Marc, I'm sure Rich didn't kill Aunt Matilda. He told me she had planned to give him the deed to her property that night, but he said she died before she could. He said he panicked and ran away." Carla stopped to breathe.

Marc looked at her. "What are you trying to say, Dr. Watson?"

"Just this, my dear fellow. Would he kill her before he got the deed?"

"I wouldn't want to dampen your theory, Watson, but how do you know he didn't get the deed?"

"You're right, of course. I only have his word for it."

Carla pulled him to his feet. "Come over here and hold me close while I try to remember other things you should know." He sat beside her on the couch.

"That's a simple order," he smiled, "and easy to obey."

"The other day after Rich left, Gladys opened up and told all," Carla continued. "Rich Preston had his name changed because he didn't want his prison record to interfere with his business activities. He planned to keep it all from Penny and me. Then, Gladys let it slip that he was up in Central City at the time of Aunt Matilda's death." She looked into his eyes.

"But, darling, your aunt was in love with him. He knew it, and I think he loved her, too."

"Was he with her when she died?" asked Marc.

"I don't know. I had just asked him how she died when we heard a car and went to the window. I knew the car. It was the third time I'd seen it—once, on the way to Idaho Springs the third of July; then again, the day before Penny's wedding."

Marc looked surprised.

"I didn't get a chance to tell you about that. Mr. Barker had me abducted and brought to his ranch house—wanted to know why I decided not to sell my property."

Marc interrupted. "Carla, why did you keep these things from me? I didn't realize you were in danger. And what about George?

You said you didn't trust him? Why?"

"I found out he knows about the ring. It's a secret organization called The Hunters. He belongs to it. So does Rich."

"Did he say what they do in the organization?"

"Yes, he did. George said they are assigned to a job and if they perform it satisfactorily, they are in line for more responsible jobs, until they are eventually earning fabulous amounts. George said he expected to have a Cadillac soon."

"But did he say how they get their money?"

"Rich let me know more about that. He said the members are instructed to get wealthy women to enlist their protective service. After the women have signed a contract, as long as the utmost discretion is used, the agent is free to use any means he sees fit to swindle his particular client out of her life's savings, or whatever else is worthwhile . . . such as a deed to an estate."

Marc got up, took a deep breath and looked at his watch. "It looks to me like this case is about wrapped up, Dr. Watson. Except for a few loose ends like: Cecil Barker's role, George's activities, the whereabouts of the deed . . . and the all important question, How did she die?"

"We've barely touched the surface then, Mr. Holmes."

"Precisely. Without the deed to the Winthrop Estate, the will can be held in Probate Court indefinitely. In the hands of the wrong person, names can be forged." Marc shook his head.

"I still can't believe Aunt Matilda would consent to letting go of her beloved Winthrop House."

He folded Carla in his arms. "I've been so thoughtless, Little Peanut. You've been talking too much."

Carla laughed at him. "Who's been talking too much?"

"And another thing, I don't want you to stay here alone. Can you go up to Irene's until I get back? I should be back by Wednesday."

"Don't worry about me, darling. I'm not alone. Besides, I have some business to take care of before you come back. I'd like to go up to Winthrop House when you do."

After seeing Marc off to the airport, Carla returned to an empty

136

house. What could she do by herself all day on Sunday? It was ten o'clock. She was tired from lack of sleep the night before, but she didn't want to go back to bed. Maybe she'd go to church.

Irene had told her to be careful before she joined a church. "Be sure they preach the Bible," she had warned. She knew Penny's church was all right.

She changed to a white linen suit, locked all the doors, and a few minutes later walked into the little church on time.

The words of the hymns came alive with meaning. The sermon encouraged her and gave new zeal to her already zealous heart. At the invitation, she went forward. Ray's folks welcomed her with tears in their eyes.

On her way home after the service, she sang aloud the words, "Calling today, calling today, Jesus is tenderly calling today."

George's Chevy was parked in front of her house when she got home. The front door was open. He must have used the key she forgot to ask him for. Seated in a big chair, a drink in his hand, he jumped up when Carla came in.

"Hope you don't mind, Sis. I brought your key back. Where'd you go? Church?"

Carla nodded and brushed by him on her way to her room, questions tumbling in her mind. George had never been presumptuous before. This was an act of invading her privacy. Had he gone home last night? If not, where had he been? Why was he here now?

"I'll be going now, Sis. Sorry I bothered you."

"Wait, George. You didn't bother me. Let's have dinner together someplace."

"I'd better not. I'm already in the doghouse. I didn't go home last night. Irene and I don't have anything in common anymore." He looked wistfully at Carla. "I don't have anything in common with anyone now."

"I'm sorry, George. Really I am." Carla touched his cheek as he went out the door. Poor guy. So alone, so miserable, so ambitious.

Late Sunday afternoon, the police chief called.

"Mrs. Preston, we have Ronald Powell in custody. We'll need your identification of him and signed charges. We'll hold him overnight. First thing in the morning will be all right."

Relief was mixed with pity. Marc would be glad to learn of Rich's capture.

18

Songs of joy and thanksgiving filled Carla Preston's waking thoughts. Jesus Christ was real. She was confident of that. This new life was wonderful—and exciting. What would today bring?

She didn't have long to wait. Jim's voice came over the phone before she was out of bed.

"Mornin', honey. Now don't say no before you hear what I have to say. I gotta see you. At The Hideaway for lunch?"

This last meeting with Jim was inevitable.

"I'll be there at twelve-thirty, Jim."

"You will? Great!"

In a gesture of finality, she put the receiver down.

She wandered from one room in the house to the other. No bustling noises, banging doors, constant chatter. Tears slipped down her cheeks. Oh, the wasted years she could have given to Penny!

Marc's call came at just the right time. She was about to sink into her old ways of remorse and depression.

"Marc, darling, you're safe! I expected to hear from you last night. I understand. How's your mother? Oh, good—then you'll be back Wednesday? No, I wasn't afraid. Slept like a baby—in the arms of Jesus. You're not jealous are you? Marc, they've got Rich in custody at the city jail. I have to go down this morning and identify him as the man who attacked me. I know it's necessary, but it'll be hard.

"Your mother gave you added evidence against him? I'll be anxious to hear about it. And before you hang up, Marc, darling, first let me say, I love you. Then, I want you to know I'm meeting Jim for lunch for the last time. Thanks, darling, I knew you'd understand. 'Bye, now."

Later, at police headquarters, in a white sleeveless shift, white sandals, hair caught up with a royal blue scarf, Carla Preston looked like a schoolgirl. She hoped she wouldn't have to face Rich Preston, but as soon as she was seated he was brought in.

"Is this the man?" the officer intoned.

Carla lowered her eyes, and under her breath she said, "I'm sorry, Rich."

That was all. Outside, she shivered in the midday heat. That desperate, hopeless man—those pleading eyes. Aunt Matilda would have grieved for him.

A few minutes later, roaring down the narrow, tree-lined road to The Hideaway, Carla was brought back to the next item on the agenda. Many secret meetings with Jim crowded her mind. This little lane always meant that soon she'd be in his arms again. Today was different.

Soon it would be over. She'd be free. Ever since her decision for Christ she had known she'd have to face this issue with Jim. The only remorse she had today was that she'd let herself get into a situation like this in the first place.

He was standing by the tall lilac hedge. He opened the car door, pulled her out and wrapped her in his arms.

"My little honey. I've missed the feel of you."

Carla gently freed herself, took his arm and guided him into the tavern. At the same high-walled booth, vivid memories stabbed her heart.

"Do you still love me, honey?" he pleaded. "It's been so long. Why do you keep me in suspense?"

"Jim, I have something important to say to you. Please try to understand."

He reached for her hands, fear mirrored in his eyes. Her words came slowly.

"We've been wrong, Jim. We've hurt Sue. How can we ever make up for that? The least we can do is to stop hurting her now."

"Wait a minute, honey. I don't understand this kind of talk. Are you telling me to make up with Sue?"

"It's not what I'm saying that counts anymore, Jim. It's what God wants us to do. Listen to me. I'll try to make you understand. You see, I've just learned that God has forgiven me of all my sins. Don't take me wrong. I'm no better than the worst kind of sinner, but I've been forgiven. But not without a price. Oh, I didn't pay for it. Jesus paid it all—He died for all those horrible sins of mine. He took the punishment I deserve. Do you understand, Jim?"

"I've never heard you talk like this before. What's come over you?"

"I'm trying to tell you. It's real. Jesus died for you, too. Can you believe that?"

"I can tell you're sure serious. You're a lot different. I can think it over."

"You do understand why I can't go back to that, since He did so much for me?"

"So this is where you are, Carla, my dear." The words hissed in her ear. Mr. Barker's bulky mass cast a shadow on the table.

Startled, she moved to the corner of the booth. In the dimness of the lamp-lit tavern, she detected a glint of madness in his beady eyes. His small white hand clutched the edge of the table.

"You think you've been putting something over on me, don't you? I've known about this young man a long time. I knew you were in his room at your brother-in-law's motel that day."

Carla saw Jim glare at Mr. Barker. "How would you like to leave now?" he said. "We don't like insults." He slid out of the booth and towered over Cecil Barker, whose eyes never left Carla's face.

"You've made a fool of me once too often," he hissed. "No one can do that to Cecil Barker."

He wheeled around, and with amazing swiftness, disappeared through the door.

Jim sat on her side of the booth. "What does he mean?"

"I don't know. But Jim I don't want you to get involved in this. Mr. Barker thinks he has a score to settle with me. He knows I'm not afraid of him. I told him the other day I was in Someone else's hands now."

"You sound so weird, Carla. Can a person change that much?" He tousled his blond curls. "Just the same, I'll follow you into town."

At her car, Jim held her hand to his cheek. He didn't try to kiss her, but looked at her with longing. It was a poignant moment for Carla. This was the last time she and Jim would have a rendezvous.

Down the dusty little road, Carla was aware of a sudden release of spirit. The break with Jim had lifted a heavy weight. Now she was free, free to look into the future . . . with Marc. She'd learned a lesson: to follow Jesus meant to forsake all known sins.

The next lesson to be learned was to put her complete trust in the Lord Jesus for all her fears. The fear of staying alone at night loomed over her like a giant to be conquered. She must find something from God's Word to help her overcome this fear.

With Barker's ominous threat still sounding in her ears, she wondered what she'd have to face in the near future. She must not panic at their next meeting.

The telephone was ringing as Carla came in the door. It was the chief of police again. She was to go immediately to her shop. Mrs. Toby, the lady who was taking her place, had called the police after the men left.

Bewildered, Carla jumped in her car. What did it mean? After what men left?

Mrs. Toby was white-faced. "I didn't know what to do, Mrs. Preston. I hadn't heard that you were selling your merchandise. These men just came in and started packing each piece in cartons."

"Did they show you a requisition slip?" asked the officer in charge of the case.

"No. They both looked so matter-of-fact, yet stern. I thought they knew what they were doing."

"Describe them, please."

"Nondescript. Average height. White, middle-aged."

"That's all right, dear Mrs. Toby." Carla put her arm around her shoulder.

"It isn't her fault, Officer. I have an idea what's behind it all, but I can't prove it. I need a little more time. I'll contact my insurance company."

When the officer left, Carla wandered about her little exotic gifts shop, noting the stripped shelves. A few items remained, such as imports from China and Japan, but all her unique gifts, the most precious and rarest ones, had been removed.

She considered the seriousness of the theft, and was unable to explain her lack of concern. Before she met Christ, she would have been in hysterics. Each purchase had been so much a part of her. Now it dawned on her she must have been an idol worshiper.

Material things had meant so much before. Now, Jesus had changed her sense of values.

Back home, Carla took a leisurely shower, slipped into her robe and, since it was too early to go to bed, she determined to look into the Bible. She longed to know Jesus better. Marc had told her to read the Gospel of John first.

Flipping through the pages, her eyes fell on II Timothy 1:7: "For God hath not given us the spirit of fear; but of power, and of love, and of a sound mind." That's the verse Irene had shown her.

Her eyes skipped across the page to verse twelve. The last half of it said, " . . . for I know whom I have believed, and am persuaded that he is able to keep that which I have committed unto him against that day."

She had committed her life to Christ. Of course, He'd keep her safe. She found the Gospel of John and read until her eyes lost their power to focus. It was dark when she got up from the big chair and went to the kitchen for a bite to eat.

At nine o'clock she got in bed and opened her Bible again. When Marc called he said, "I hope you weren't asleep."

"Oh, no, darling. I've been reading the most wonderful things about Jesus. The Gospel of John, like you said. But listen to this." She flipped back to II Timothy and read the passages that had impressed her. "Do you think it would be all right if I underline those verses, so I can remember what they mean to me?"

"Of course, Little Peanut." She knew his eyes twinkled. "I'm glad you're reading your Bible. That's the only way you can know Him."

"Oh, I almost forgot. Someone walked into my shop today and packed and walked out with all my most valuable gifts. Mrs. Toby thought they had permission. I think I know who is responsible, but there's no proof. I'll wait 'til you get here. You'll know what I should do."

"You don't sound very upset about it, Carla."

"I know. Isn't it strange? Material things don't seem to mean so much anymore."

"My Little Peanut, you are truly a child of God."

"I know it, but Marc, my darling, I need your flesh and blood arms around me, too. Please hurry home."

"That's what I wanted to tell you. I'm leaving this evening. I'll drive 'til I'm too sleepy, then hit the road early in the morning. I should be in Englewood by late afternoon. After I rest awhile, we can have dinner together."

"How wonderful, Marc!" she squealed. "I'll have a home-cooked meal ready."

"No, no. I'm not sure when I'll be there. You just be ready. We'll go up to Idaho Springs."

"I'll call Irene when I get through with you," she laughed.

"Plan to stay awhile. I want you on hand when we bring this investigation to a close. I'll tell you everything when I see you. I love you, Little Peanut, more than the spoken word."

She smiled and snuggled down in the covers.

The next afternoon, Carla's heart leaped across her breast at the sound of Marc's car in the driveway. With no pretense of modesty, she ran out to meet him, threw her arms around his neck, and in broad daylight, he kissed her repeatedly, until they heard the neighbor's children giggling over the fence. They both waved at the children and ran into the house.

"It looks like you're ready to go." Marc laughed at the row of luggage.

"Sit down and rest awhile." Carla pulled him to the couch, and put a pillow behind his head. "Wait here 'til I get our coffee."

Carla gave Marc the details of the theft of her merchandise.

"You said you think you know who did it?"

"I'm sure. But there's no proof. The description of the men is on file at headquarters. What else should I do?"

"Nothing, right now. We have enough to keep us busy for the next few days. Do you want to know about my new evidence, Dr. Watson?"

"How thoughtless of me, Holmes, old fellow. Proceed."

"Very well, Watson. By the strangest coincidence, my mother has a very dear friend, a mystery writer, who keeps old newspaper clippings on criminal cases in her reference file."

"Oh, how handy!"

"My mother just happened to mention that her sister had been swindled by a charming man she had met while at my mother's home. The friend remembered a similar case in Los Angeles, rushed home and brought back the clipping."

Marc hesitated.

"Go on," said Carla. "I know what you're going to say."

"The man's name was Richard Preston. After several old ladies testified against him, he was found guilty and sentenced to two years in prison."

"Gladys told me about that."

"The point is, my mother recognized him as the man who came to Aunt Matilda's farewell party. He called himself Ronald Powell. She remembered he said he was with an insurance company, but, the thing that impressed her was Aunt Matilda's attraction to him. She told my mother later that he was an older image of her fiance. Most amazing of all, both their names were Ronald."

"Aunt Matilda was probably living in a world of fantasy," said Carla. "She thought she loved Ronald Powell. That's why she was willing to turn over the deed to him."

"Precisely, Dr. Watson."

"But, how did she die, Holmes? And where is the deed? Who ransacked Aunt Matilda's room? What were they looking for? And, whose ring did we find?"

"It's still a puzzle, isn't it, Little Peanut?"

They sipped their coffee in silence. Carla broke the silence. "What about the money Rich swindled from her? Will you be able to get it back?"

"There's a possibility we'll get some of it. The Los Angeles Police Department identified Ronald Powell as the same Richard Preston they have in their files. By the way, the Los Angeles police have requested Ronald Powell be arraigned in Central City where he will be charged with fraud in connection with swindling my aunt."

Carla shivered. "I can't help but feel sorry for him, Marc. He's a sensitive man. I think he loved her, too."

"You said that before, Little Peanut. You're a hopeless romanticist, along with everything else adorable."

After Carla was settled in her foom at Grant's Haven in Idaho Springs, Marc promised he'd be back at nine o'clock to tell her goodnight.

"And keep your door locked. Don't open it for anyone."

Carla unpacked her large bags and hung her clothes on hangers. Irene had said she wouldn't be over because she and their mother were going to prayer meeting. She knew Marc wouldn't be gone too long, but it seemed so lonely by herself. She tried to settle down to reading her Bible, but her mind seemed to wander. When she heard a light tap at the door, she thought it could be Marc.

"Who is it?" she called. At George's familiar voice she opened the door and let him in.

19

George staggered to a chair, flopped down and stared at Carla. "Well, how's Sis this fine evening?"

She had seen George a few times after too many drinks, but not like this. He seemed different—shrewd—evasive.

"Don't worry about me," he muttered. "I'm okay—but you're not. Got yourself in a lot of trouble, didn't you? Nobody can fool around with the Chief."

"George, what are you talking about?"

"As if you didn't know," he sneered. "You're in for it, Sis. And I'm the one assigned to do the job."

"What kind of job?" whispered Carla.

"Wouldn't you like to know? 'Smy assignment. Gonna be a full-fledged Hunter."

Where was all that peace she had before in the face of danger? George had been assigned to kill her. Could he really go through with it? If she could just stall him for ten minutes, Marc might come back in time.

"George, I know how much the Hunters mean to you. Before you do anything, could I ask you a few questions? Then, I promise I won't scream or put up a fight."

"You're sure a cool one. What do you want to know?"

"It's about Matilda Winthrop. How did she die?"

George ran his hands through his hair and frowned.

"I guess it won't hurt anything. You won't be able to tell anyone anyway."

Carla waited, breathlessly, and prayed for time and facts.

"I don't know exactly how she died. My assignment was to keep an eye on Powell. His job was to get the deed, not to make love to the old lady. Barker was suspicious of him . . ."

"What does Mr. Barker have to do with all this?"

"Oh, no you don't." George leered at her. "You thought you could catch me off guard." His eyes seemed to glaze over. He shook his head as if trying to clear it.

"I won't tell anybody about the Chief Hunter. I know what'd happen if I did."

"What would happen, George?" she said, softly.

"Poof! Snuffed out by the Hunters!"

"Oh, George, what dangerous game are you in?" She put her arm over his shoulder.

He leaped to his feet and shoved her on the bed. Falling over on her, his heavy chest crushed her ribs. The next thing she knew, she was trying to breathe through a pillow held roughly over her face. She heard his muffled words. "Don't fight it."

With superhuman strength, she thrust her knees upward, finding their mark in his side. She heard him gasp. At the same time the pillow fell from her face. She bolted upright, knocking him to the floor. He grabbed his side and groaned.

He seemed to regain some of his senses. "What happened? Oh, Sis—I didn't do it, did I? He told me to kill you. I didn't, did I? No, no, I couldn't do it." He rocked back and forth, his hands over his head.

There was an urgent pounding at the door. Carla let Marc in.

"Thank God, you're safe! In here, Officer."

He shielded her in his arms as a policeman bounded in, lifted George to his feet and looked at Carla. "You all right, ma'am?"

She nodded, feebly, as he took George away. "Marc, how did you know?"

"Are you sure you're all right now? They want us to go back to headquarters. They're bringing Barker in. Preston spilled everything. They'll want a statement from you too, Little Peanut."

"Everything is happening too fast! Do mother and Irene know yet?"

"I think it's best to wait for all the details. It looks pretty bad for George, at this point."

"I don't think he's done anything really wrong yet, Marc. He's so weak when it comes to money. I don't believe he could have gone through with it."

"Through with what?"

"With killing me. Didn't you know?"

"Killing you? No. Preston said they'd probably kidnap you and threaten you if you told anything you knew."

"George said he'd been assigned to kill me."

"Try to forget it, Little Peanut. I'm not leaving you again until they're all in jail."

At headquarters, Carla came face to face with Cecil Barker. It was hard to recognize the cringing picture of terror. The desk sergeant questioned her about his character and what he had done in regard to complaints she had recorded. She reviewed the two abductions and the illegal seizure of her valuable merchandise.

"That will be all for tonight." Carla breathed normally again when Mr. Barker was led through clanging doors to the city jail.

"I want you two to be at Winthrop House in the morning before eight," the sergeant told them. "Powell and Grant will give their versions of events on the night of Matilda Winthrop's death. And I want the Kerneys on hand, too."

Marc nodded and propelled Carla to the car.

"Your mother and sister won't miss you tonight, will they?"

"I doubt if they'll try to rouse me before nine in the morning. Why?

"I can't rest with you out of my sight—and I'm tired."

"What are you suggesting, Mr. Randall?" Carla smiled.

"Spend the night at Winthrop House with me." She could hear laughter in his voice.

"Why, Mr. Randall, I hardly know you."

"And I promise, you won't know me any better in the morning."

"All right. Since you are a man of your word, I consent."

He went to the motel room with her. "You might want a few personals, whatever women need."

Carla opened the door of her room and pointed to her overnight bag. "Everything's in there, I think." He picked it up, stepped out and waited for her to lock her door. Why didn't she feel guilty?

On the drive to Central City and on up to Winthrop House, they spoke very little. Carla knew Marc must be exhausted. As they entered the front door, the grandfather clock chimed eleven times.

"Where would you like me to put this?" He indicated her bag. She watched his eyes sweep up the wide stairway.

"Aunt Matilda's room?" She was excited.

"If you like." He took her hand and led her upstairs. He put her case on the bed. "Get into something comfortable. I'll do the same. My room is next door if you need me. Meet me at the top of the stairs in ten minutes."

Carla slipped into her royal-blue robe. She didn't feel guilty. He'd seen her in the robe before, the night Rich Preston knocked her out.

She dismissed the unpleasant thought, brushed her hair and let it hang on her shoulders. She rinsed her face, added a little blush, then a dash of cologne, and stepped out the door to the stairway.

From the balcony, her eyes swept once more to the far end of the house, through the intimate dining room, and back to the familiar living room. She didn't hear his step behind her. His arms went about her waist, his chin rested on her head.

"My Little Peanut, I love you." Turning around to face him, she saw a new light in his eyes.

"I've got to tell you what I think the Lord is doing. A vision of this estate, idle and wasted, has haunted me this past week. Then, the Lord let me see what could be done with it. It seemed to be all laid out. A Christian Conference grounds."

His words came faster.

"There's a section west of the house that's ideal for it. A stream, crystal clear, stocked with trout, runs through a rich meadow. Dormitories could be built, and even a hotel for older people who can't rough it."

He stopped, looked deep into her eyes, cupped her face in his hands and lingeringly kissed her. Still holding her face, he said, "By the way, have I asked you to marry me?"

Carla's throat tickled. "I thought you'd get around to it."

Portraying an old world lover, Marc deliberately brought from his jacket pocket a folded hankerchief, spread it on the floor, and knelt.

Taking her hand, he raised it to his lips. "My lady, I love you with a heart overflowing. You would make me the happiest of men if you would consent to give me your hand in marriage."

Carla giggled. "Just my hand, sir?"

He leaped to his feet and crushed her to his chest.

"What is your answer, woman?"

She struggled free, and with eyes lowered, "Oh, dear, this is so sudden. I had an answer all prepared. It has completely slipped my mind."

Tenderly and soberly, he held her head to his chest again. "Your answer means everything to me. I've loved you since the first time I saw you. I mean it, Little Peanut."

"Oh, Marc, you know it has to be yes!"

Down the long stairway, her hand tucked under his arm, they moved dreamily across the living room to the stereo. Marc selected a record, and soon the lovely strains of a waltz floated through the room.

"This is the record they were dancing to that night. Sarah remembered it."

Moments passed as he held her face close to his and gazed into her eyes. Then he whispered, "They're like liquid pools of moonlight."

"And yours are twinkling star-clusters." She slipped her arms around his neck and pulled his head down for her kiss. "I love you with all my heart," she said simply.

They strolled over to the fireplace. He lit the logs and looked toward the long silk cord. "I'm afraid there'd be no answer. Wonder if there's anything to eat in the kitchen?"

Carla's heart skipped across her breast. She was going to help in his kitchen. It would be like being mistress of Winthrop House.

With a tray of food and hot chocolate, they came back to the living room, and sat on the floor by the coffee table.

"We're engaged," Carla whispered.

Marc leaped to his feet. "Isn't there supposed to be a little token to seal the promise?" Taking the stairs three steps at a time, he was back almost immediately.

Her dropped beside her, lifted the ring from the velvet box, and slipped it on her finger. He kissed the tips of her fingers, then held her hand out in front of her.

"It's the most beautiful diamond I've ever seen," Carla whispered.

He dropped the velvet box in her hand and waited. "Have you

guessed yet?"

Her hand shook as she gazed at the faded lavender box. "It was he s," she said.

Je nodded. "Aunt Matilda gave it to me on my twenty-first birthday. Said it was for the girl I chose for my wife."

"Oh, Marc, I feel so special!"

He lifted her to her feet and held her close. "You are," he said, then pulled her down on the couch, his eyes closed, head resting on the back.

"I know you must be tired, my darling," said Carla. "Why don't you stretch out?" With his head on her lap, she rested her head on the back of the couch and was soon fast asleep.

Her next observation was the light of dawn sparkling through the stained glass in the front door. Her legs were numb, her shoulders ached. Marc began to stir, rubbed his eyes and sat up.

"Did I use you for a pillow all night, my Little Peanut?" He stretched his arms and legs and pulled the silk cord.

Sarah stood in the little doorway. "Mr. Randall?" Surprise showed in her voice. "When did you get here?"

"Last night, Sarah. Got a cup of coffee for two sleepy people?" Carla expected a grunt from her.

"Will you be havin' breakfast, too?" she asked.

"Later, after we wash up a bit. Just coffee now, please."

In a moment she was back, poured two cups of coffee and set the server down. "Ring when you're ready for breakfast."

Close beside him, Carla was acutely aware of steaming coffee, freshly crackling logs, and Marc's loving presence.

"This is more than my heart can hold," she exclaimed.

"It makes my head swim," he stated flatly.

Back in Matilda's room, Carla showered and dressed and marveled again at the comforting atmosphere.

Marc was waiting when she came downstairs. "Your sister called. I think she's worried. I told her you'd call."

After talking briefly with Irene, she told Marc, "They know about George now. She's taking it well. So is mother. They're trying to raise bail. She said the police are on their way up here with George and Rich. She hadn't missed me until a little while ago."

"Are you ready to face all this, Little Peanut?"

"I'll be glad to get all the loose ends together." Carla shivered.

"Let's go over some of those loose ends before they get here, or do you want breakfast first?"

"I don't," said Carla. She poured more coffee and sat on the hassock at Marc's knees. He took his little black book from his pocket.

"I guess the most important question is, how and where did Aunt Matilda die? Then, how much money did she give Ronald Powell? And—where is the money, now?"

"And," continued Carla, "we want to know, how did he become involved with Barker's agency? And—what kind of hold does Barker have on the members of the Hunters?"

"And—where is the deed to Winthrop Estate?" Marc grinned. "Is that a conflict of interest?"

Carla sipped her coffee. "Quite understandable, my dear." She probed her mind for other questions.

"Oh, yes—who forced his way in and ransacked Aunt Matilda's room? And—how did that ring get in the jewel box? And—who does the ring belong to?"

"Slow down, my dear." Marc covered her mouth with his in a long, firm kiss. "That should do it."

She closed her eyes and offered her lips to him again. "I don't have anything else to say."

20

Marc brought extra chairs into the living room to accommodate those who were to take part in the testimony of Ronald Powell and George Grant. They, along with Cecil Barker and all other members of the Hunters, were still in custody, pending evidence yet to be established in the case.

The police sergeant and two deputies accompanied the two men. Walt and Sarah Kerney were there to substantiate Powell's statements.

Marc took advantage of the informality of the gathering, and as future owner of Winthrop Estate, opened the meeting with prayer to God. He asked for truth to be established and justice to be done.

The sergeant began in a matter-of-fact tone. "This is not a court of law, but I must inform you that what you say here can and will be used as evidence against you. Since you both have agreed to give your version of the night Matilda Winthrop died, your testimonies will be held in strict confidence until the trial starts."

He leaned back in the big chair, put his hands on the arms and nodded to Rich Preston.

"We have the proof of the legality of your name change from Richard Preston to Ronald Powell. It won't be necessary to go into that at this time. What we want now is an accurate account of the time you spent here with Matilda Winthrop the night she died. Please begin."

Carla's eyes stung with tears as she watched Rich Preston's flushed face and hopeless expression.

"I'll have to go back to the night I first met Miss Matilda Winthrop. It was a farewell party given by her sister in Beverly Hills, California. I had been assigned to contact her as a future client for our protective agency. It was my job to persuade her with my charm."

"May I interrupt?" said Marc. "How did you become involved with the agency?"

"I heard of them from my cellmate. He'd been with the Hunters, but was serving a short term for a crime not connected with them. He said Cecil Barker was a man of power and intelligence, and would give me an excellent opportunity. He had ways of knowing of my special talents—with older women." His smile was twisted.

"Continue with events of the night in question," commanded the sergeant.

"Yes, sir. There's one more point I'd like to mention. Matilda Winthrop was outwardly attracted to me from the very first. I learned later that I reminded her of her fiance who was killed the day before they were to be married, some fifty years before. She told me he would have looked just like me if he'd lived. And his name was Ronald." Rich Preston looked embarrassed.

"I admit I took advantage of the opportunity. I got her to sign the contract with the promise I'd visit her at Winthrop House as soon as I could get away. Cecil Barker knew I was seeing her and warned me to be discreet. By that time Matilda had showered me with gifts, even large sums of money."

To Marc he said, "It's all banked in my personal account in California. After that terrible night, I decided to return it to her heirs as soon as possible."

Marc gave a curt nod.

"That night was to be our last night. I let Gladys, my wife, know that my business in Central City would be finished by the end of the week, and she was to meet me in Denver. I gave her Matilda's address without thinking. She dropped a note there for me. I'm sure you have it. It was missing from my belongings when I got home."

The sergeant interrupted in a loud whisper.

"Are you getting all this down?" he asked his deputy. "Continue, Mr. Powell."

"Well, Matilda was becoming increasingly possessive and seemed to be going backward in time. In fact, she was convinced that last night was her wedding night. I couldn't hurt her—I went along with the fantasy all evening. She was completely absorbed in the past."

His eyes begged Marc for understanding.

"She wore her wedding gown and her feet were so tiny in those

155

high heels with the rhinestone buckles. Truthfully, I was completely charmed by her beauty and coquetry, and the sweet fragrance of violets."

Carla's tears flowed down her cheeks. How sad! Rich really loved her.

He coughed, wiped his forehead with a handkerchief and continued. "We wined and dined and danced all evening. I don't know how late it was. While we danced near the stairs, she whispered her love for me and told me to wait and—like a young girl—she ran up those stairs . . ."

Rich stepped to the newel post and looked up. Carla knew he was reliving those last moments.

"I waited here . . ." he whispered.

"You'll have to speak louder," said the sergeant.

Carla saw him swallow. "It was right here. She came down the stairs—like a queen. It must have been her wedding nightgown—it was yellowed with age—but she was beautiful." He gulped and daubed his face again with his handkerchief.

"When I took her in my arms, I heard a soft sigh. She went limp. I don't know how long I held her on the steps. I knew she was dead. I was too stunned to move. When I looked at her face, there was a little smile on her lips."

To Marc, he whispered, "I'm sure she was happy."

Marc held Carla close while she sobbed uncontrollably.

Rich ended his testimony quickly. "I rushed out, panic-stricken, fled to Denver, picked up Gladys, turned in the rented car, and flew back to Beverly Hills."

"Thank you, Mr. Powell. You may be seated."

Now it was George's turn. His usually ruddy cheeks were pale.

"I was assigned to watch Powell that night. Barker expected him to get the deed to Winthrop Estate. The Kerneys were to witness the signing. It was my job to see that Powell didn't leave with the signed document. I waited all evening for him to come out. It must have been one o'clock when he rushed out and, without closing the door behind him, hopped into his Cadillac and roared away." He looked at the group with frightened eyes.

"It looked funny to me, so I took a peek in, since the door was open anyway. No one was in sight. I tiptoed over to the stairway.

156

It was there I saw her—leaning against the post, relaxed. She looked like she was asleep."

George sounded like he had the whole account memorized. Would he ever take a breath?

"I cleared my throat real loud," he went on. "I watched to see if she heard me. Then I realized she couldn't hear anything. When I thought of Powell, how he rushed out, I was sure he'd killed her." George was careful to avoid the eyes of Rich Preston.

"As I thought of the consequences, I knew something had to be done to keep Barker and the Hunters out of it. Before I realized what I was doing, I carried her upstairs and took her in the room with the open door. I thought I could make it look like she died a natural death, since she was so old. I just put her in bed, like she died in her sleep."

He looked embarrassed, clasped his hands together, and looked at the policeman from under his brows. "I guess she didn't look that natural."

Before he resumed, George took a piece of paper from his pocket, walked across the room and gave the deed to Marc. "I think you've been wondering where this was."

"How did you get it?" asked Marc.

"After I got the lady settled on her bed, I looked around and there it was on her night stand. I saw it wasn't signed, but, looking ahead, I thought I could probably get it forged. I told Barker later that Powell must have gotten away with it after all."

He breathed a long sigh. "There must be a better way to make a living."

"Tell us about the forced entry," said the officer.

"Oh, that. It was necessary that I find my ring. It must have slipped off when I laid her out. I didn't want Barker to know I'd been in the house. If my ring was found there, I would have had a hard time explaining to him."

George looked pleadingly at Carla. "I'm really sorry about last night, Sis. That was when I realized Cecil Barker had gone too far. He was letting personal feelings interfere with business. I didn't know he was that ruthless. I want you to know, Carla, I'm turning state's evidence against him."

He shook his head, took a deep breath and said, "Maybe

Irene's way is best."

"There's one more question that comes to my mind," said Marc. "How did the ring get in my aunt's jewel box, and who hid it back of all the shoe boxes?"

"I did that, Mr. Randall." Sarah spoke up. "I found the ring on the floor next to her bed that mornin'. It looked interestin', and I thought it might be valuable, so I dropped it in her jewel box. Then, I got the idee, if nobody asked about the jewels, me and Walt'd have somethin' to fall back on in case we'd have to move away from here. 'Course when you asked for the jewel box, I gave it to ya right away."

"Think no more of it, Sarah. You've both been loyal for many years. You can stay on as long as you want to."

"Thank you, sir . . . and ma'am." She nodded at Carla.

At last, Sarah had accepted her.

The next few weeks were trying, but Carla was happy just to be near Marc. He helped her with legal matters, like the transfer of her house to Penny and Ray, who were both enthusiastically grateful and planned to live there. He hastened the process of retrieving her merchandise from Mr. Barker's apartment in Central City.

"We'll store the pieces at Winthrop House, Little Peanut, and when you have more time, you can display them the way you like."

He was a rock to lean on at the trial. It had been brief. George had turned state's evidence and was given immunity. Rich was found guilty of swindling and received a two-year sentence. Cecil Barker's sentence for fraud and conspiracy to commit murder, was the maximum. All the members of the Hunters received heavy fines for fraudulent practices.

A week of joyous activity succeeded the wearing days of the trial.

"Irene, you and mother have to help me. Who should I invite to the wedding?"

"Why don't you let our church secretary put an invitation to the congregation in the bulletin?"

"That sounds all right to me. Will you take care of it?"

"Oh, Sis, I think it's so romantic to be married at Winthrop House. I'm glad Sarah likes you, now. She'll arrange all the refreshments for the reception, I'm sure."

"Marc told me just to let Sarah know what I'd like to have. Even the decorations would be done by the florist. I really don't have to do a thing—but wait."

"That's good! You're too scatterbrained, anyway."

Marc Randall was occupied with opening his law office in Central City, but every evening was spent with Carla.

One memorable evening, he took her to the hotel dining room where they first met. After their meal, he took a white satin case from his pocket.

"Just a tiny preview. You can look, but not touch." He held a slim circlet between his thumb and forefinger. The candlelight dazzled from it.

"I've never seen a ring like it, Marc!" She looked at it closely. "It looks like one diamond formed in a circle."

"They are baguettes," Marc smiled at her delight.

She held up her finger with the diamond from Aunt Matilda. "Won't they be beautiful together?"

The most eventful night of Carla's life finally came. Irene helped her get dressed. In Aunt Matilda's room, she slipped into Aunt Matilda's wedding gown. As Irene hooked eyes, Carla bubbled.

"I've never been in love before, Irene. Everything's so right. I'm sure Jesus makes the difference."

Irene smiled and placed the crown of real orange blossoms on her head, a gift from Marc's mother. On top of a small white Bible, she placed Marc's nosegay of violets.

"Don't forget this." Irene lifted the tall crystal stopper from his special gift of French Violette Parfum.

Carla descended the stairs alone. The stereo played the wedding march; Marc met her at the foot of the stairs. She had never seen him so handsome, dressed in a white formal tuxedo. The young pastor of the little church in Idaho Springs performed the ceremony, elegant in its simplicity.

At last, the guests were leaving. Carla's heart beat faster with each Goodbye, God bless you. The Kerneys had retired long before. When Marc closed and locked the door, they both leaned against it and sighed. Then, with her hand tucked under his arm, they moved to the foot of the stairs.

Facing her, with her hands in his, he bowed his head. "O Lord, I thank You with all my heart for my beautiful wife."

As he held her tenderly, her eyes followed each stairstep to the top. The memory of that nightmare was present for just a fleeting moment before her thoughts came back to him. This man at her side was no shadow. She was confident he would not disappear when they reached the top of the stairs.

At that moment, she caught a glimpse of eyes that twinkled nd dashed up the grand